VISIONS

AND

NIGHTMARES

A. F. Stewart

Visions and Nightmares

A. F. Stewart

Copyright © 2020 by A. F. Stewart.

All rights reserved.

Editing by Proof Positive

Cover design by A. F. Stewart

Original artwork licensed by Adobe Stock Photos

Interior photos courtesy of Pixabay and licensed by Adobe Stock Photos

ISBN: 978-1-9990659-6-6

Nightmare

Night shudders against the undertow

In-between the fragile heartbeats

Galvanized towards byzantine monsters

Hiding, smiling in the obfuscous layers

Those insinuating seconds, taunting,

Masked from banal extant reality

Awaiting the imperfection moment

Revelation, alteration, the infinity of—

Enmity, totality, malevolent mentality

Contents

Blood on the Looking Glass
(or Alice Kills Wonderland)

"We're all mad here," said Alice.

She shifted her feet, her heels clicking on bone, and carefully stepped across the giant skulls, leaving tracks on their charred surface. She smiled, remembering how they died, how the flames licked at their writhing bodies, how the blood flowed from their wounds.

They died screaming, just the way she liked it.

Alice raised her face to the sky as the rain started, laughing as the drops wet her skin and drenched her clothes. She inhaled deeply of fumes and burnt flesh as the patter of rain drummed discordant music against the dead. Beyond

the corpses, the drops sizzled as water met the embers o
the still smouldering earth, sending more smoke drifting
in the air.

Alice inhaled again, the scent tickling her nostrils. "Burn
it all down. That's what I'll do." She giggled. "I'm coming
for you, Red Queen, and you Rabbit, and you Hatter. I'm
coming for you all."

She marched forward, dislodging her sword from an eye
socket as she went, and climbed down from the mound o
bones. She hopped to the scorched earth and paused. The
sun radiated off the barren landscape, bright light filling
the empty space between her and a copse of gnarled, singed
trees. Alice gazed towards those waiting woods, a menacing
smile playing on her lips.

"I see you, bird. Go tell her I'm coming."

Alice slashed her hand across her throat in a cutting
motion, before swinging her sword above her head. She found
the remains of the path and skipped towards the woodland.

⁜

One of the Red Queen's raven army huddled in

cadaverous tree, the images of the giants' massacre tumbling their horror around in its brain. It watched Alice grow closer and closer, before it flew off to report to its mistress.

From the ruins of the giants' grasslands it flew, winging over the Dark Forest and the royal flower gardens, above the chess fields and over the river until it reached the palace of the Red Queen. Its mistress waited, and the bird landed on her outstretched gloved hand.

It cawed once, and then spoke, "Wonderland has fallen, my liege. The Hatter and Rabbit spoke true. Their lands are a smouldering wasteland, and the Queen of Hearts was beheaded by Alice. She killed the March Hare. I believe she roasted him and ate him; all I found were the remains of a cookfire and his skin." It ruffled its feathers and shuddered. "I do not know what became of the rest of the inhabitants. Perhaps they fled to this realm, or other strange corners to hide."

"And now she is here?" A melancholy danced with the Red Queen's words.

The raven nodded. "She has destroyed the giants.

Nothing is left of their home or the edges of the woodland. I fear the Dark Forest shall soon burn as well."

"I fear we shall all burn," replied the Red Queen. "Go join the rest of your kind while I tell the others she has arrived."

The Red Queen watched the bird fly away before returning to the confines of her palace. She went to the conservatory, where she found the White Rabbit and the Hatter. The latter was pacing the checkered floor and whirled when she entered the room.

"You have news?"

"She has arrived. The giants are dead and she is headed to the Dark Forest."

The Hatter shuddered. "We must raise an army to stop her! You must summon the White Queen, gather your combined forces!"

The Red Queen stared at the Hatter, sorrow in her eyes. "The White Queen fled days after you brought us the news of Alice's rampage in Wonderland. She took most of our forces with her. And there will be no help from the Queen of Hearts. She is dead."

The Hatter groaned. "How many remain?"

"We are all that's left. The three of us and my ravens."

The Hatter trembled, flopping into a chair. His voice cracked as he replied, "No. It can't be. That's not enough." A small moan escaped him. "We should have never brought her here. Never sent her there. But—but…" He moaned again.

The Red Queen sighed. "We had no choice. The Jabberwocky… We had to do what we did. But all is not lost. We still have time. She's still Alice."

"No." The White Rabbit whimpered, his ears twitching. "Time's run out. Time is lost." He looked at the Red Queen, his whiskers quivering. "She took my watch." He held out a cauterized stump missing a paw. "Cut it clean off. But she didn't take my head. Not yet." He tucked his injured limb down by his side. "Not yet."

✳

Alice moved through the Dark Forest, searching the trees. Each footstep withered the foliage and the air rained with dead leaves. Well off the path, in the middle of the woodland's shadowy heart, she walked into a clearing and stopped.

"You can't hide." She looked up at a slender birch tree. Its lower greenery desiccated and flaked off as she stared. "I see you, Cat."

"Hello, Alice." The voice drifted softly, the tone shaky. "Good to see an old friend." High in the branches, a feline head poked out with a hopeful smile.

Alice met its Cheshire grin with one of her own. "I missed you in Wonderland, but here you are."

"Here I am. Minding my own business." The cat grinned wider, its voice gentle. "The picture of innocence. Not the sort to get in your way. Not worth your time. Not like the Duchess. She deserved what you did." The cat purred. "We can still be friends."

"I don't think we were ever friends." Alice sighed. "And you're not innocent, are you? None of you are."

"I never meant any harm!" The cat meowed loudly, pleading. "None of us did!"

"But you did. Harm me, I mean. Now you face the consequences." She scowled at the creature.

The cat backed up the branch, trying to hide. "I'm not

worth your time, truly I'm not."

"Now that's for me to decide, isn't it?" Alice raised her sword and waggled the tip at the cat. She chuckled as her blade glowed, the metal becoming red hot. "Naughty, naughty cat. Time to die."

Alice swung the weapon, felling the tree in one stroke, cutting through the wood like soft butter. She jumped back to avoid the trunk as the tree crashed down.

The cat tried to leap away before it hit the ground but tangled itself in the branches. Alice plunged her blade into its neck and the Cheshire Cat died, its grin forever frozen on its face. Alice bent down and lifted the carcass by its scruff. She tossed it to a patch of bare ground and lopped off its tail, stuffing the grisly trophy in her bag next to a shrivelled rabbit paw, dried mouse tail, a dodo beak, and the withered ear of a hare.

She walked around the fallen tree and travelled out of the woods, embers smouldering the ground in her wake. When she exited the forest, the vegetation behind her burst into flames and the Dark Forest burned.

Alice continued her journey, humming a gentle tune.

The Red Queen stood on a palace balcony watching the woodland burn in the distance. The Hatter and the Rabbit had fled hours before, running again to escape Alice for a few more days, and she ordered her raven army to do the same. It broke her heart to see the birds fly away, but she knew they would at least live, if only for a little while longer.

The battle is between us now, Alice, as it should be. Much of this is my doing, my responsibility. I must face the monster I helped create.

Alice walked onto the chess meadows with a smile. Behind her, fields of living flowers screamed, their petals and stems burning in a fiery conflagration of her rage. The Red Queen waited on the other side of the black and white board carved into the grass.

"Hello, Alice."

Alice stopped, staring at her enemy. She let out a sigh.

"So, you've come to meet me again. Good. Have the

Hatter and the Rabbit joined you this time?"

The Red Queen shook her head. "They ran when they heard you arrived."

Alice chuckled. "I'm not surprised. They were ever the cowards. I'll find them soon enough."

"Why? Why all this destruction? It doesn't have to be this way."

"Doesn't it? What choice do I have anymore? This is all I have left."

"No." The Red Queen held out her hand. "I offer you another choice. Let me help you."

Alice tilted her head, her face melting into a confused expression. "Help me? You made me. All your mind games, your manipulations. You, the Hatter, Rabbit, and all the rest turned my childhood into a surreal circus. For what? To kill a monster?" Alice sneered. "But it didn't work out, did it?"

The Red Queen dropped her hand. "We never meant to hurt you. We only wanted to survive. We needed you."

"Oh yes. You made that oh so clear. Only me. The saviour of Wonderland and all the realms beyond. You never told me there would be consequences. All you said was take the sword and save us all." Alice held up her blade, embers falling from the metal.

"We didn't understand. Not then. When the sword spoke your name, we sought you out. We focused on the fact that you would be the one, you would harness the power and kill the creature. We feared the Jabberwocky and it blinded us to other ramifications."

"Did it now, this fear of the Jabberwocky? Perhaps, though, you would have been better off with it than me. And you say you didn't understand. Perhaps. Yet you were careless. Reckless. The sword showed me the truth of things. It spoke my name because it knew me. But you didn't have to listen. You shouldn't have listened."

The Red Queen hung her head, her shoulders slumped, shame in her eyes. "I'm sorry. We wronged you. I ask forgiveness. I let fear rule me."

Alice clucked her tongue. "The queen was ruled, was she? By her terror of things unknown? By the cowards and liars surrounding her? By her own mistakes and foibles? Is that your excuse?"

"I have no excuse. I did what I did. But time has afforded me clarity."

"What clarity would that be? That you could have intervened before it was too late? That you could have stopped the White Rabbit from bringing me here? But you thought you needed me, didn't you? To undo your mistake. To reset time."

"Undo what mistake? I don't know what you are talking about. I wish there had been another way. I wish I could turn back the clock and reset everything. But time is a peculiar thing, Alice. It only runs one way."

Alice laughed and spun around on one foot. "I know all about peculiar things, my queen. But you are wrong. Time runs in all directions. I know that now." She stopped spinning and smiled. "For you see, there are no more ticks on the clock for me. They all fell off and flew away." Alice hopped forward a step. "I am, I was, I've never been. Lost and shattered through time. Pieces scooped up and put back in the wrong order. A thousand bees humming in my head. Flashes of pictures showing me awful things."

"I'm sorry. That was never my intention."

"Maybe, maybe, but it is the result. And that is what matters. Here, now, and even then. All the same and written in blood."

The Red Queen stared at Alice, desperation etched on her face. "It doesn't have to be, it doesn't—"

"It does! That's what I'm telling you!" Alice roared to the world, and the ground shook with her fury. "Don't you understand? It has already happened. You just need to catch up." Alice hopped from white square to white square until she stood a foot away from the Red Queen. "This happened the moment you opened the door. The moment you convinced the White Rabbit to lure me to Wonderland." Alice shook her finger at the Red Queen. "Naughty, naughty queen. You broke time. You created the Jabberwocky. You created me."

The Red Queen whispered, "I don't understand."

"No, you don't, and you didn't. All the same thing now. That silly, silly thing. A thing in the past you could have prevented, and this you cannot."

Alice lifted her sword, pointing it at the Red Queen.

"Listen well while I tell a story." She smiled. "Once upon a time, a monster came and you were afraid. Did you wonder where it came from? No. Just, '*kill it, kill the Jabberwocky,*' came the cry. So the sad, confused queen looked and looked for a saviour and found poor little me. Poor gullible Alice, waiting for adventure. So I came when you called, ate up your lies and your fun and all the false friends. When you asked, I took up the sword and marched off to war." Alice turned the blade to catch her reflection and the reflection of the Red Queen.

"I swear I didn't know it would drive you insane! The sword wasn't supposed to do that!"

Alice laughed. "Is that what you think? No, my queen. The sword is not responsible for who I am now. You are. The sword only whispered the truth as I killed the Jabberwocky. As I killed the creature with my own face. That I am, I was, the Jabberwocky."

The Red Queen gasped. "No! That's impossible!"

Alice shook her head. "Remember. I said time runs in all directions. I will become the Jabberwocky that was, just as

I was the Alice that killed the Jabberwocky me. Opening the door to Wonderland created ripples upon ripples and things folded onto themselves."

The Red Queen repeated, "It's impossible!"

Alice laughed. "Oh no, it's possible. Believe. Indeed, believe. At least six impossible things before breakfast."

The Red Queen screamed, "Why are you doing this?"

Alice sighed. "I am doing what has been done. The Jabberwocky has lived and died. I have lived and died. We, they, will do so again. I have stood here before. I have stood beneath your castle. It has happened and will happen. We are caught, my queen, you and I, in a loop. A forever loop of death and life, of monsters. You and I, forever monsters."

"No!" The Red Queen took a step forward, the point of Alice's sword pressing against her chest. "Not if you stop."

"Oh, silly Queen. I can't stop." Alice leaned forward and whispered in the queen's ear. "The Jabberwocky, me, told me all her secrets as she died. As I died. I'm just a ghost, you see. Her, my, dying wish played out."

"But if you don't continue, you won't—"

"You still don't understand!" Alice's scream rattled the earth and caused the wind to howl like a wounded wolf. "There is no stopping! It has already happened! I killed myself! I took the sword and slew the Jabberwocky, stared at my own face taking my last breath. Do you have any idea what that feels like?"

The Red Queen shook her head.

"What plays out now is an eternal inevitability. We are the architects of our destruction, you and I. We destroy everything in the worlds beyond. It has happened, it will happen again, over and over in an eternal circle. Living, dying, forever and ever. We are caught. There is no escape."

The Red Queen straightened her spine and raised her chin. She closed her eyes.

"Then so be it."

Alice smiled and pulled back her sword. She plunged it into flesh and the Red Queen burned. In screams and a blazing conflagration she burned, an immolation that reverberated across all the worlds. In her final moments time slowed, and she saw Alice move on, saw her blaze a path of destruction to ignite the remainder of the realms beyond. With her last breath the Red Queen tasted the end, witnessed reality turn to blackened ash, including her own flesh. And then *tick, tick, tick,* the clock unwound to begin the cycle again.

"We're all mad here," said Alice.

A Life for a Life

I counted the blooms of mauve-coloured heather growing on a small hillock, anything to avoid gazing upon the open grave and its wooden coffin. The corpse of my love nestled in that unconsecrated ground, a brave and gentle man lost to me forever.

A hand fell on my shoulder. "Come away, Isobel, 'tis unseemly of you to be here."

I scowled and turned my head to my husband, Alasdair, but said nothing. I allowed him to lead me away from Callum's resting place. I heard thumps of dirt shovelled onto the coffin and that heart-breaking echo followed us.

As we walked, my husband kept his firm hand on my

shoulder, and his voice whispered in my ear. "'Tis a hard thing, but you reap what you sow, Isobel. Do not make it worse for yourself by bringing scandal to our house—more than you already have, at least. I've managed only just to hush the gossip and lay the blame on that reprobate you took as a lover. Try anything against me again, and you'll join him in the grave."

I bit my tongue to stop the bitter retort. If he had been a good husband, I would not have strayed nor tried to kill him to free myself. But the blame is mine. Not for the murderous attempt but its failure, and my mistakes causing Callum to hang for the crime.

I cast my thoughts back to that night. My anguish, my hatred and Callum's distressed face as he tried in vain to dissuade me from my desperate violent scheme. He tried to warn me. I wish I had listened.

"Please, Isobel. I understand your humiliation at what he's done to you, and your rage. I share that anger, but this isn't the way. Killing him is not the answer."

"You cannot understand. Killing him is the only way."

"We'll run away together. To France or to Ireland. Far away from his reach."

"His reach has little limit, as does his pride. He will not stomach being publically deserted or being branded a cuckold. He'll hunt us and kill us both. I'm not merely seeking revenge. I'm defending our lives, my love."

The truth to be certain, yet my defence, my plan lacked power, and Callum paid the price. It would not be a mistake I'd make again.

I glanced at my husband's face. Strong, weathered and stern with no hint of the cruelty hiding just under his skin. He knew how to hurt me, where to hit my body and where to wound my soul. I turned my gaze away and stared down the path leading back to the village.

He's made an oversight in his strategy this time. He's left me with nothing to lose. I'll send him to Hell, even if I have to join him.

I straightened my spine and shoulders and kept silent as the grave until I walked through the front door of my home and prison.

Well past the midnight hour, my husband snoring in our bed, I climbed from beneath the quilt and left the bedroom. I crept to my sewing room, to a small trunk tucked in a corner. From its contents, I withdrew my mother's book and stroked the worn leather cover. To all appearances the volume seemed normal enough, a handwritten collection of recipes, cures and wifely tips, but I knew the secrets between the pages. The book in my arms, I walked to the window and sat in a chair, illuminated by the full moon.

I opened it, seeing my mother's handwriting on the yellowed parchment. I remembered her hunched at her table scrawling her notes with pen and ink. What she recorded in her book, most would consider blasphemy, but I treasured her knowledge. For my mother practiced witchcraft of a sort, hiding her spells and secrets among the commonplace recipes and advice written to aid a woman's duty.

I smiled. She would approve of what I planned. More than a few men had fallen to her hand over the years.

I should have done it this way from the beginning. If I had, Callum might still be alive.

I turned the pages to the correct spot in the book and read the words by the moonlight.

How to Bargain with the Faerie.

The faerie are dangerous, capricious creatures, and any contract with them will come at considerable cost, possibly your own life. They have no great liking for humans, and even if summoned may not bargain. The gift you offer must be of value and, at least to them, outweigh the cost of what you ask. And above all, do not trick them or cheat them.

I rubbed the page with my thumb, suddenly worried. No chance of my cheating them, if they could give me what I would require, but what could I offer them?

Faerie prize little of what humans possess. Some will take silver or gold for small favours, such as a potion or minor glamour.

Silver and gold I did not have, and I asked no small favour in any case.

For the desperate, though, there is a way. But the cost is high and not for the righteous.

I smiled. Desperate, I was, and willing to give most anything.

The faerie will bargain in blood. A life for a favour. Give them a life, a human soul, and they will do most anything in return. But beware, once the bargain is sealed, do not renege. Or they will take your own soul as payment.

I laughed softly on reading the words. A soul I had to give, and a perfect one in return for the bargain I needed. I read on, studying how to summon the faerie, and then closed the book, satisfied.

It took a fortnight before Alasdair allowed me to leave

the house on my own, but as soon as he relaxed his guard I went for a woodland walk in the twilight. I took the old path to the hidden glade and the ancient stone faerie ring. Then I began my work.

I circled the outside of the ring with salt and inside with dried bluebell petals and red clover, placing a jar of honey and a bottle of my husband's whisky in the centre of the stones. I stood on the outer edge of the stones and recited the summoning.

"From the gloaming, I call, between the shadows and light. To the faerie I beseech, to help ease my plight."

I held my breath as the seconds ticked off, until the lilting sound of a harp broke the silence, and the sweet smell of strawberries drifted on the wind. The air within the ring shimmered a glowing gold, and when the light faded, a tall white-haired man stood inside the ring.

"Who summons the faerie?" He glared at me and then glanced down at the offering of honey and whisky. "At least you have sense enough to bring gifts."

I nodded. "Freely offered for your gracious boon of

listening to my plea. I am Isobel Fairbairn and I come to ask a favour. A life for a life. I wish my husband dead and will grant you the gift of a soul in exchange."

The faerie quirked an eyebrow. "A request I have not heard in a while, but one we would readily accept, if you can fulfil the bargain." The faerie looked at me with some distaste in his expression. "I have doubts that someone such as you could persuade or trick a human to give up his life to us."

"There will be no need of trickery. The life I offer has no choice. Your faerie senses can tell you that, I believe."

The faerie frowned and stared at me, bewilderment etched on his face. He closed his eyes and I felt his magic reach out towards me. When he opened his eyes, he smiled. "I see. You do indeed hold a life in your grasp. You can give us a soul and a choice one. But a cold bargain. Are you certain? Once your word is given and the pact sealed, there is no going back."

I straightened my shoulders. "I am certain. Agree to kill my husband, Alasdair, and you can have the soul you sense."

"Very well then. Meet us here three days hence in the gloaming hours."

In a whirl of light he vanished. I noticed the honey and whiskey were also gone, sighing in relief and with no regret. I would do what I must to seek my revenge. I turned away, smudging the circle of salt with my foot, knowing I would return in three days.

On the eve of the third day I returned to the woodland glade and met again with the faerie. Now I stood inside the stone fairy ring, surrounded by nine beings of the otherworld. A silver-haired woman wearing a gold pendant and flowers in her tresses stepped into the circle with me, taking my hands.

"You have asked a bargain of the faerie. Your husband's death in exchange for a soul. You have offered the rarest of all souls, the one of an unborn, unbaptized child. Will you seal the bargain?"

"I will." No going back now. "I'm ready to complete the bargain with ye. A life for a life."

I knew the price when I made my bargain. An unholy

cost, but I was already doomed to Hell for what I'd done. I'd taken an innocent life, no matter that I had meant the poison for Alasdair. Callum hanged for my crime, even after I confessed all to my husband to save him. I'd have two deaths on my conscience, but nary a regret for the third.

The faerie let go of my hands. "Then we will seal the pact in blood and take the payment." She removed a silver knife from her belt and pricked her finger. She then pricked one of my fingers and pressed them together, mingling the blood.

"The blood contract is sealed." Then the woman placed a glass jar on the ground and stepped out of the circle.

I took a breath and waited. The faerie joined hands and in unison chanted their spells, weaving a radiance of magic across the circle and through my body. It took only a few seconds for it to begin.

The pain in my gut doubled me over, and I screamed for all that I promised myself I wouldn't. The baby inside my belly thrashed, fighting for its life, and I wept. I fell to my knees and watched the child's soul ripped out by faerie magic. It spun in a gossamer light around the sacred circle, seeking escape but inevitably drawn to the jar and imprisoned. The rest was messy and bloody, painful almost beyond comprehension as I lost my child, its remains stillborn as a lump of dead flesh.

I closed my eyes as it ended, barely hearing the faerie swear their oath to fulfil the bargain. I never felt them retrieve the jar, never heard them leave, yet when I opened my eyes they were gone. Everything was gone.

I pushed myself to my hands and knees and crawled out of the circle, avoiding the tiny body. I inched my way to the shovel I brought and dug a hole in the cold ground, a grave for my child. Only then did I look at its small corpse, and only to bury it. The innocent thing deserved that much. When my sin was well and covered in dirt, I spared a thought for the child and an apology.

"I'm sorry. Nothing but a poor babe barely formed, you didn't deserve your mother's betrayal. But I had no love for you."

Not the way you came into being. Not after what Alasdair did.

Memories made me shudder. Alasdair's cold stare,

his telling me he knew about Callum. Locking me in the bedroom for months as a prisoner. And then that night. Taking his husbandly rights, he called it, and not a thought to my refusing or my resistance.

No, I couldn't bear his child after that, nor the thought of his living. This way I rid myself of both. But without Callum…

I sighed and turned for home. It would take some doing to explain away the blood and dirt, but maybe part of the truth would do. Alasdair might leave me be if I made it seem I lost our child through providence and ill fortune. At least long enough for the faerie to keep their word. That's the part I'll enjoy.

Watching that bastard die.

Glass and Stone

"If only you had your sister's beauty, Ida. You are such a plain little thing."

My father told me that often as a child. Perhaps that started my fascination with mirrors, and my mother's mirror in particular.

"Don't listen to his words." Mother always declared after Father's slights, and sometimes wiped away my tears. *"He doesn't see you. But I do, little one."* Then she smiled at me and took me to her sewing room.

We spent hours there, away from Father and my sister, Rosa. Her mirror sat in a corner of that room, not an overly fancy thing, just a black frame carved with filigree. I stole glances in its shiny surface, staring at my reflection, puzzled. I never understood why my Father hated my looks. True, I had not the pink-cheeked blonde cherub look of my sister, but I was not hideous.

So I stared in the mirror, trying to unravel that mystery. My mother sighed when she caught me looking.

"Reflections are lies, Ida, they never show the truth. For that you must travel deeper than the looking glass. Our hearts show who we truly are."

As a child, I never comprehended her words, but I remembered them. I remembered everything about her. Especially after her death.

She died when I was but nine. A fever took her soon after childbirth, aided by the grief over my stillborn baby brother. I remembered watching my father console my sister after he told her the horrible news; he sent a servant to inform me of her death. That day I began to hate them both.

After witnessing their tender scene, I ran to Mother's dressing room to hide and grieve. I don't know what possessed me, but I stole her favourite pendant, slipping it around my neck and tucking it beneath my pinafore. Then I curled in a chair and cried. No one came to find me. No one asked after me the next morning at breakfast.

Following her death, I lived as an afterthought to Father and my sister. The servants often took pity on me, though, and while the house was still in mourning, I convinced a maid to move the mirror to the room I shared with my sister. I needed to feel close to my mother. I had no one else.

For Father still doted on Rosa, still called me plain. He treated me well enough otherwise, but I knew he only loved her. It bothered me sometimes, this uneven affection, his lack of attachment to me. Rosa was little better towards me, taking her cues of behaviour from him.

Without Mother, I remained alone.

Perhaps that was why I spent my time with her mirror. I often sat in front of the glass and stared, wishing I could walk through, like in a storybook. I turned my mind inward, let my imagination play, and sometimes, if I was quiet, I thought I could hear her voice.

"Be strong, little one. I will be with you always."

I enjoyed imagining. It made me happy to hear her voice in my head.

Then one day, I heard other voices.

"Open the door, Ida. We're waiting."

The mirrored surface shimmered for the briefest stitch in time. I glimpsed a world of green and gold, of verdant grass and splendid city spires, so beautiful. And then it vanished, and the voices silenced.

But I knew. I knew the mirror held magic.

I ran my finger over the carved frame and noticed something I hadn't before: an odd symbol. I shivered and fingered my mother's pendant. The etched mark on the mirror matched the engraving on the back of the setting.

Why did they have the same marking?

I promised myself to discover the truth, and I spent my hours from that moment searching, but I never found the answer to unlock the mirror's secrets.

Then one day, the year I turned seventeen, Father took my mirror away.

That year my sister married. She was all of nineteen years old, and a man of thirty came to take her to be his wife. I heard them talk about how he had money, a good position in society, and so arrangements were made. For months, the wedding preparations went on in our house; all fuss, flowers and lace gowns. I enjoyed it all—Rosa would finally be gone—until the day Father brought servants to the bedroom and boxed up the mirror.

I stood on one small spot of the carpet, dumbfounded and motionless in my horror. "What are you doing? Where are you taking the mirror?"

"It's to be a wedding gift for your sister. Something of your mother's for her to take to her new home."

I wanted to scream, rage, but I said nothing. He would not listen anyway. The mirror left with my sister.

My joy at seeing Rosa leave turned to ash. She triumphed yet again.

She placed the mirror in her parlour, so I saw it each time I visited, but one afternoon it seemed different, more vibrant. I puzzled why, and then, suddenly, I knew.

I confronted Rosa.

"You discovered the secret of the mirror, didn't you? That's why Father gave it to you?"

She stared at me, with her perfectly coiffed curls, and for a moment I thought she would lie. But she didn't.

"Yes. I found it. It took me a while to decipher the writing, but it was all in Grandmother's journal." She rose, strolled to the mantel and opened a cherrywood box sitting there, removing a small leather-bound book. She returned and handed it to me.

"Go ahead, read it. I'm sure you'll be amused at how close you were to its wonders, all those days staring at it. Did you think you were going mad when it used to shimmer?"

I quivered; I couldn't keep my fury and anticipation from spilling over. I hugged the book to my chest, the weight of it pressing against Mother's pendant. "You saw the magic as well?"

"Of course I did! You didn't think you were special did you? All of Mother's bloodline can see the magic. I was just smart enough to figure it out."

You mean Father gave you access to Mother's things. Gave you the key to the trunk where he locked away her keepsakes.

I said none of that aloud. "Have you seen what the mirror holds? What is it? What is that beautiful scene it showed?"

"Of course I've seen it, you ninny! It's a portal to another world, and I've been there many times. You wouldn't believe where it leads to, such a beautiful and exciting place. Such splendour and freedom."

"Would you show me?"

She frowned and curled her fingers. She looked at the mirror and glanced back to me. "I don't know, you're so—so plain. You wouldn't fit in."

"Please." I kept my tone pleading and soft. "Just one look."

Rosa sighed but replied, "All right. But only a quick look."

"That's fine."

We went to the mirror and my sister touched the symbol on the frame, and then the glass. She spoke two words in Latin.

"Aperire terram."

The mirror's surface rippled like tossing a rock in a

pond, then melted into silver liquid suspended in the frame. Slowly, what was once glass played out a scene of a golden city, a thing of heavenly beauty. I smiled, a wistful grin, grateful for a small glimpse of my dream.

Then Rosa whispered, "Vivere memento."

The magic vanished and only a mirror remained. I cried out, a gasp of disappointment that slipped past my lips and immediately regretted the unguarded moment. I heard Rosa chuckle.

Then she surprised me.

"Keep the journal for a week. Read it. See what our heritage truly comprises, what you missed."

I clutched the journal tighter and nodded, my eyes fixed on the mirror.

I will not let Rosa win.

Yet I only smiled and said, "Thank you."

⁘

For the next seven days I immersed myself in the pages of my grandmother's journal, reading all about the secrets of the mirror. Rosa spoke true when she called it a portal, but it led to not one world but an infinity of worlds. My sister obviously failed to read the journal thoroughly. If she had, she might not have let me have it, for to access some of those worlds something else was needed.

My mother's pendant.

I smiled as I devoured the knowledge, knowing now what I must do. At the end of the week I was ready and returned to my sister's house. We went to the parlour, where I gave her back the journal. I glanced at the mirror and smiled before I sat down.

"It was a fascinating read. I understand everything now."

"Then you understand why I must be the keeper of our family legacy. We are the guardians of the mirror. Gatekeepers to the world beyond the glass. I can't just let anyone through. They have to be the right sort. The highest quality."

I nodded. "I understand. Grandmother was quite adamant that only the strictest of moral character be given custody of the mirror." My conscience twitched at those words. What I planned would not meet with her approval, of that I was certain. Yet I continued. "Such a responsibility would be beyond me, safeguarding all those infinite worlds from the unworthy. It must be very taxing."

Rosa laughed. "Hardly. Father and I are the only ones who know…well, now you, so—wait. Did you say worlds?"

I smiled, just a hint. I had her now. "Yes. Didn't you know? The journal describes many worlds beyond the mirror, ones with riches and beauty past imagining." I paused, feigning my best innocent expression. "I thought you read it?"

"Well, I did, mostly." Rosa bit her lip and fidgeted in her chair. "At least the parts about using the mirror."

As I suspected, she fell into old habits. As a child, she only read parts of her lessons, badgering me to help her instead of doing the work herself. This time she failed to read the remainder of the instructions and the small list of Latin phrases in the back of the journal. She read what interested her and ignored the rest. Her mistake.

I acted surprised. "You have explored none of the other worlds?"

"No." Rosa frowned, and I saw the irritation on her face.

"How do I see these other worlds? Tell me."

"It would be easier to show you. It involves other symbols on the mirror." At least some of them did. Others, well…she would see soon enough. I rose. "Come to the mirror."

I allowed Rosa to pass me and walk ahead. She never noticed me pick up the heavy brass candlestick from the table. She saw the blow that smashed her in the head, though. Rosa turned as I swung and slammed the candlestick into her lovely face. I'll remember her look of shock forever, and I will treasure it always.

Rosa crumbled into an ungainly heap at the foot of the mirror. There wasn't much blood, but I wiped up what little seeped from her wound with my handkerchief, and I cleaned the base of the candlestick before replacing it on the table.

As my sister groaned from the floor, I pressed the symbol on the mirror frame, then placed my right hand on the glass as I touched the matching symbol on the pendant.

I glanced down at Rosa and said, "Facilis descensus averno."

This time the mirror's surface rippled and dissolved into a crimson liquid, snapping like embers in a fireplace. I felt the heat against my skin and snatched my hand away.

I bent down and heaved Rosa's body through the mirror into the hellish world that lay beyond. As she fell, I laughed, seeing dark shadowy creatures race to greet her. They caught her and dragged her off to what I hoped was some hideous fate. I'm sure she would have screamed, had she been fully conscious.

Then I whispered, "Vivere memento."

The magic ended, the portal closed, leaving only my reflection in the glass. For the first time in my life I liked what I saw in the mirror.

In the confusion and scandal that followed my sister's disappearance, I retrieved the mirror from her house, convincing her outraged husband to give it to me. It stood in my room until Father married me off a few months later. I think he may have suspected something; possibly he just wanted to be rid of me. At least my husband is an amiable man, content to leave me to my own devices. The mirror now stands in my own sewing room, as it once did Mother's.

Do I have any regrets? Not a one.

I'm glad I did what I did. Rosa was a liar and a thief, stealing my father's love from me. I hated her. Now *my* mirror stands in *my* home, a reminder of my only happy memory of Rosa. Of the day I destroyed her.

Now, if only I could devise the same fate for Father...

Magicks

Zenna screamed as another tattoo burned its way across her skin. In that moment it did not matter that her spell saved a coastal town from a tidal wave. She only felt the aftermath of pain the magic caused. She held her throbbing arm and sobbed as wrinkles formed around her eyes and another lock of hair turned grey.

More of my life stolen.

Zenna collapsed, her body curling into a ball, the cold wood floor pressed against her skin. She let the tears flow, batting away the hands of worried priestesses trying to comfort her. She ignored all the anxious pleadings and offers of help, weeping until she had nothing left to cry. Then she let her guardians help her to her feet and lead her down the narrow temple hallways towards her room.

Halfway there, she changed her mind and twisted out of their grasp, her breath coming in pants. "No, no, take me to the altar room. I wish to pray."

The priestesses bowed and escorted her to the prayer room. With a curt nod she dismissed her handlers and they left. Zenna turned to the wooden altar adorned with a carved image of Crthysis, the god of magic. She could see the night sky and the stars through the round window above.

She stumbled the few steps forward and sank to her knees on one of the cushioned prayer stools. She held out her hands in front of her face, turning them as she stared at the shrivelled skin and wrinkles covered in dark umber tattoos.

"Why do you take my life in exchange for your power? I am your vessel, yet you strip me of who I am piece by piece and mark my flesh with each use. I do not understand."

"You will soon enough."

Zenna gritted her teeth against the voice echoing in

her head. Always the same answer to her question. No matter how many times she asked.

"When I die, you mean."

"Yes."

She sighed, and her eyes darted to the last remaining bare spot of skin on her arm, on her entire body. She closed her eyes.

"One tattoo left to appear. One spell left. Then I will have my answers?"

"Yes. You will know the truth."

Zenna opened her eyes and slowly rose to her feet, wincing at the twinges in her back and knees. She turned from the altar, the sense of betrayal she felt from the moment she cast her first spell rising in her heart. She hobbled towards the door.

One more spell and I die. I've never even lived. I may not even see my twenty-first birthday.

With a sigh, Zenna opened the door and allowed the priestesses to take her back to her bedroom.

Back within the confines of her private sanctuary,

Zenna eased herself down on her bed. She lay on her side, curling her arms around her knees, and rested her head on the pillow. She stared at the familiar wall, her stomach churning in fear and disgust.

It hasn't changed in all these years. Nothing has changed.

She knew every inch of this temple, its walls her prison since the age of nine. And soon it would be her tomb, her body laid to rest in the crypt and her successor occupying her bed.

"I hate this place. I've always hated this place." Her whisper filled the room with her pain.

"You should hate it. Hold on to that hate as you die."

Zenna laughed, her tone and volume tingeing the sound with a hysterical edge. "The gods want me to hate, whispering such words in my ears, while the priestesses want me to have blind faith and love the world more than my own life. Who should I believe?"

"The priestesses lie."

Zenna sucked in her breath. "Why do you say that? They are your loyal servants. They serve your will."

"Do they? Are you sure?"

"What do you mean?" Zenna demanded an answer, but the voices remained silent. She frowned and fretted, but she heard nothing more. She finally closed her eyes and fell asleep.

A gentle shaking woke her the next morning, and she opened her eyes to see two familiar faces staring down at her: her guardian priestesses, her own personal jailors. They smiled.

The tallest of the pair, Ysa, spoke. "Breakfast awaits you in the garden. Allow Dralla and me to escort you. Afterwards you can bathe and change into fresh clothing."

Zenna grimaced. Allow indeed; she had no choice. Yet food, a bath, and new clothes would be welcome. She glanced down at what she wore. She hadn't even changed to her nightdress but slept in her robes from yesterday.

"Take me to the garden."

The two women bowed and helped her to her feet. They assisted her as she walked the corridors, and then through the archway to the open indoor garden. Zenna breathed in the fresh air, the only small piece of nature she had known for years.

"I remember as a child running through the grass to a

river. It seems so long ago, a lifetime."

"Yes, Your Holiness, before the gods graced us with your presence. Praise them, that they rescued you and sent you here to serve."

Zenna clenched her jaw. *Curse them, you mean, and their faithful soldiers who kidnapped me and locked me away here to die.*

The anger trickled through her blood and bone as the priestesses settled her onto the prepared couch, fluffing pillows and tucking a blanket around her as if she were a sick child. Then they brought her fresh warm bread slathered in butter, sweet slices of fruit, and honeyed oatcakes sprinkled in crushed nuts. She ate, the food soothing the edge off her mood.

Zenna closed her eyes, relaxing and shutting out the sight of the adoring faces of her guardian priestesses. She knew they believed her divinely inspired and themselves privileged to serve her. Most days she wanted to scream at them and call them fools.

She steadied her breathing, an even in and out, letting her

mind wander, picturing images of grassy fields and sunlight. She could almost feel the breeze on her face, hear the—

Her eyes opened abruptly. "Do you hear the sound of marching, of horses?" Zenna frowned, strange sounds crowding her ears. "I smell…" Her body stiffened, muscles going rigid in the sudden throes of second sight.

Her eyes rolled, white translucent film fading their green colour, while her mind and senses travelled on a wave of magic. The vision connected into her brain and she became a ghost on the edge of infinity, shifting across present time into future sight. She saw the vast armies standing opposite across a great field, the banners of Sheiwen and Bryka waving underneath dark clouds of a threatening storm. She smelled the metallic tang in the air from armour and weapons, the stink of nervous sweat and the hint of evergreen from the trees.

In moments, the battle unfolded, the armies charged, engaged, men killed and died until the air turned to the stench of blood and bile, of death. Shouts and screams roared across the field and the conflict reverberated with the distant echoes of thunder. When the rain finally came, it turned the earth to sloppy red mud and washed the feathers of the carrion birds feasting on the entrails and eyes of the dead. She saw Sheiwen defeated and the invading army of Bryka marching on her homeland.

Zenna's sight returned, and she found herself staring into the faces of the two priestesses. "An invasion is imminent!" The words tumbled out, though she knew speaking them meant her death. "The armies of Bryka are coming!"

"You must stop them, Your Holiness!" The two priestesses screeched, jumping to their feet. They helped Zenna to stand and rushed her to the Chamber of Spells. As they dragged her along the halls, nausea rolled in Zenna's stomach, the aftereffects of the vision threatening to heave her breakfast over the marble floors. The priestesses paid no heed to her gagging and mewls of protest, sweeping her into the chamber and depositing her on the cushions in front of the scrying bowl and dais.

"Stay here," Ysa snapped to Dralla, "I must warn the High Mother and fetch her to witness this. You must help Her Holiness begin the preparations for her spells. She must stop the invading army before it is too late!"

Ysa rushed from the chamber, leaving a determined Dralla and an unsettled Zenna alone in the chamber. Zenna heard the lock click and knew escape was impossible.

She sighed. "Bring me the scrying oil."

Dralla dutifully fetched the bottle of sacred oil, and Zenna poured a few drops into the water of the bowl and swirled the two together. A few drops of oil clung to her tattoos, reminding her of the consequences of her actions.

I will save lives, destroy others, and die in the process. What does it all mean? Does it even have a meaning?

She wondered if she would have her answers in death, in the glorious afterlife the temple promised. In her heart she doubted it; another one of their lies. With another sigh, she stared into the water.

Zenna spoke one word, "Feroq."

Images rippled on the surface, iridescent shapes emerging from the oil, a scene of the present. She saw the Sheiwen army encamped near the border, but no sign of the Bryka forces.

"We are in time. The Bryka warriors are still marching,

I think. They have not crossed the borders yet."

"What next, Your Holiness? Do we wait for the High Mother?"

"No. Bring me the jars marked 'essence of alim' and 'tincture of rosel'."

"As you wish." She scurried over to the shelf of prepared potions and returned with the required items.

Zenna took the jars and placed them by her knee. She focused her attention back on the scrying bowl, swirling the water again and whispering, "Siroq."

The scene shifted to beyond the border and she glimpsed the vast Bryka army, hundreds of men strong. Far greater than the Sheiwen encampment of soldiers.

"The invaders are on the Dawlei road, heading south through the mountains. They will have to march through the Fai Pass to cross the border. This is where I can stop them."

As the words left her lips, she heard the lock click open, and the High Mother rushed into the chamber.

"Have you found them?" The High Mother moved to her side.

"I have." Zenna stared up at the leader of the temple. There would be no escape now, even if she had entertained the hope. The High Mother would break her if necessary. "I will perform the Storm Flare spell."

The High Mother smiled, her posture relaxing. "Good. An excellent choice."

"I ask one favour, though, as this will be my last tattoo." Zenna dared one last squeak of bravado. "Take me home to be buried. I do not wish my bones to rest in the temple crypt."

Zenna heard a gasp from Ysa and almost quavered under the High Mother's frown, but she stared them all down. Finally the High Mother nodded.

"I will arrange it. May your soul find the gods."

Zenna sighed and picked up the two jars, gazing once again into the scrying bowl. She watched as the Bryka army approached the Fai Pass. She poured two dollops of the powdered alim into the water where it coated the surface of the liquid, before seeping below the vision scene etched across the bowl. Zenna then poured in the tincture of rosel, and it spread a film over the water. She let it settle and closed her eyes.

Zenna pictured the army moving towards the pass, a blue sprinkling of alim powder falling from the sky followed by a rain of perfumed rosel. She hummed and intoned a vibrant chant, attended by her shouted words.

"Arquis cekkil pashtiq maresderwyn!"

For an instant time suspended before the scrying bowl erupted in flame and the room filled with the echo of faraway screams. Zenna opened her eyes and looked down. The vision in the water showed charred and smouldering bones and piles of glowing ash where an army once stood.

She said softly, "It is done," before she screamed in pain as her last tattoo etched itself into her arm. As she watched helplessly, the last bit of dark ink appeared and a great pain blossomed in her chest. Then her heart stopped beating.

"Welcome home, child, blood of demons. We have been waiting for you."

Zenna opened eyes no longer contained within a physical body. She looked down at her hands, now tattoo free and darkly translucent. She stood in a cavern of red stone, pillars reaching towards a vaulted ceiling. In the dim light she saw hundreds of gossamer figures surrounding her.

"You're the voices." She nearly jumped at the sound of her own voice. It sounded different. Harsher, deeper, but somehow comforting.

"We are. We are the Dreyal. The ones called demons in the world you left behind."

"Demons? Not gods?" Zenna felt the shock of the biggest lie race through her.

"There are no gods. Only magic users and those without the blood."

She could not believe that. "What of Crthysis? His worship? Everything they taught me?"

"Crthysis was a Dreyal. The great betrayer. He conspired with the unblooded to enslave the spirits of all Dreyal. He fused magic with death and bound our race to serve the temples. We were once free creatures, free to use magic without consequence. Now we are fated to die, and our history and memories are sullied with the taint of demon."

"But I don't..." Zenna wanted to say she didn't believe, but she did. "It was all a lie. Everything, from start to the end."

"It was. It is. But your life and sacrifice was not in vain. All Dreyal served a greater purpose. To achieve our freedom again. Come to us now, child, join your true brethren and fight the lie. Fight to free the souls of the Dreyal. You are the last piece."

The figure who spoke to her held out a hand and she felt the pull. She moved forward, could not resist the call, the beckoning of her spirit. She stepped into the welcoming fold, taking her place among the Dreyal. The ground and air shook, sparks slicing her surroundings.

"What is happening?"

"We are ready to return to the world. To break the curse of Crthysis. You are last. No more children will die to serve magic."

For a moment Zenna saw the face of the young girl who replaced her in the temple.

"She will not die for her talent. She will no longer be enslaved. You have saved her life, if not your own."

"I don't understand."

"We have united. We are power. Power enough to rise. To

erode the chains that bind our magicks and imprison us. This day we are strong enough to return to their world. Today the demons will be free."

In a flash of light, the spirits ascended back to the mortal world. And the war for demon kind began.

Connection

As she came around the bend in the road, Annalisa hauled on the reins, slowly bringing her horse and wagon to a stop. From her perch on the high wooden seat she gazed at the valley below and the township nestled there. The afternoon sun cast a pretty glow over the scene, creating an idyllic view.

"It looks like a nice place, doesn't it, Pebble? Better than that crumbling tower we just passed." The horse whinnied at the sound of her voice. "Our new home. Eastwych." She liked the way the name rolled off her tongue. "Not too small, not so big that you could lose yourself. Things will be different here, better." She flicked the reins and her cart rambled down the road, towards her place to begin anew, her place to leave the past behind.

She hummed to herself as the wheels bounced against the hard-packed dirt, keeping time with their clacking. She smiled when she entered into the town, past the stone walls and through the wooden gates. The dirt road turned to cobblestones, and she wheeled by the two-storey wooden gatehouse with a wave to the guards, to turn on to a road marked High Street. She gawked as she moved along, peering at the gardens, the decorated buildings and houses, happy to have arrived. She manoeuvred down High Street to the town square, where she pulled on the reins and brought her wagon to a stop.

"You a trader?" a voice called from a shop to her left, and Annalisa glanced in its direction. A tall, handsome man owned the voice, a man with broad shoulders and tousled dark hair.

She smiled, her heart doing a small flutter and her voice giddy. "No, I'm your new healer. I'm supposed to meet with a Thomas Madder at the Eastwych Hall."

"Just a little way down the street, that big wooden building." He pointed at a large timber frame structure. "That's the hall. Thomas should be there. If not, should be someone there to tell you where he is. I'm Gregor, by the way, the town carpenter." He walked over and held out his hand to her.

A slight nervous giggle escaped her, as she shook his offered hand. "Lovely to meet you, Gregor." She regretted the laugh and hoped it didn't make her seem like a simpering fool. "I'm Annalisa. Thank you for the directions."

"Any time, always glad to help."

She nodded in farewell and snapped the reins, her mind a muddle of sweet distraction. Pebble moved sharply and the cart jerked forward, giving Annalisa a jolt. She ducked her blushing face in embarrassment as she drove on to the hall.

Annalisa pulled the wagon off to the side of the road as near to the building as she could manage, climbed down and tied off the reins to a hitching post. She gave Pebble a pat and went inside.

Lit candles shimmered in wall sconces, casting a dim

glow within the building, helped little by the sunlight peeking through the small, dirty windows. At the far end—past a long wooden table with several high-backed chairs—stood a group of five people. Annalisa made her way towards them, her boots beating echoes on the planked floor with every step. She waved as they watched her approach.

"I'm looking for Thomas Madder? I'm the new healer for the town, Annalisa Baudry."

"Oh, wonderful, wonderful. You've arrived. I'm Thomas Madder." A portly, smiling gentleman with thinning red hair and wearing a scarlet tunic a bit too tight for his girth waddled up to her and grasped her hand. He pumped it vigorously in a handshake, babbling and beaming as he did.

"Oh, you can't imagine how wonderful it is to have you here at last. We've been without a healer for so long, let alone one with magical abilities. How was your trip? Oh, I expect it was wonderful, the land in these parts is so lovely this time of year. And the roads so well maintained. Not like in the rainy season where everything can get a bit muddy." He put a hand behind her elbow and steered her towards the rest of the gathered people. "Let me present you to everyone."

Thrust forward and encircled by strangers, Annalisa put on a cheerful face and dutifully shook hands as Thomas made introductions.

"Everyone here is on the town council. This is Rose, our baker," Thomas began. Annalisa nodded to a petite older woman with intense blue eyes. "Cyril, the blacksmith." The firm handshake left her fingers tingling. "Henry, our town barber." She resisted the urge to wipe her fingers from his clammy touch. "And Emeline, our metalsmith and jeweller." The willowy woman barely grasped her hand in greeting.

"It's so lovely to meet you all." Annalisa flashed her dimples and her most gracious smile.

"That's who you hired, Thomas?" The metalsmith, Emeline, cast her a harsh look. "Let's hope her skills are more impressive than her appearance." Behind her, the other woman, Rose, giggled.

"Behave now, that's not the way to greet newcomers," Thomas scolded. "Now that we're all acquainted, I'll show you where you're to live and work. Come, come." Thomas all but swept a bewildered Annalisa off her feet and hastened her out of the hall, whispering in her ear as they left. "Pay little mind to Emeline. She wanted her cousin hired as the town healer, and she's apt to be bitter towards you for a bit."

He paused in his rush to leave as they came to her horse and wagon. "Is this yours? Of course it is. Come on then, up we go." Thomas gave her a push and she clambered onto the seat, with him following. "I'll take the reins, I know where we're going."

Thomas Madder snapped the reins and Pebble bounded forward with a whinny and a snort. Annalisa gave a soft yelp and grabbed the edge of the seat to keep from falling off as they moved down the street at a fast clip.

"Not to worry, not to worry, I know how to handle a horse and cart." After a few twists and turns down the streets, Thomas pulled to a halt on Red Tree Lane in front of a charming white timber-frame two-storey house with a rose garden in front.

Annalisa gasped. "It's beautiful."

"It's a sturdy house, to be sure. Room for your healing

and herbal shop downstairs, living space upstairs and there's space for an herb garden in the back."

She scrambled off the wagon and hurried to the front door, tapping her foot as she waited for Thomas to follow. With a smile and a chuckle, he ambled over and produced a key, holding it out to her. She snatched it up and turned the lock, slid the bolt, lifted the latch and sprinted inside. There were benches and a long table, cupboards, a fireplace—everything she needed to set up shop. She twirled about, laughing.

"You're pleased with it then?" The jolly, booming voice of Thomas broke through her bliss and she remembered her manners.

"Yes, it's perfect. Thank you."

"Wonderful. I shall leave you to settle in, unless you'd like some help?"

"No, thank you for the offer, but I can manage."

"Good. Just come down to the hall when you're ready to open your shop, and we'll spread the word. If any need of your services should arise before then, I'll send for you."

"That's fine. It shouldn't take more than a day or two to have everything in place."

"Wonderful. Goodbye then." With a nod, Thomas left.

After Thomas departed she unharnessed Pebble, stabling him in comfort after finding, much to her delight, a roomy horse stall at the back of the house. She also found a well and the garden plot Thomas mentioned. Once she settled Pebble, she unloaded her cart and explored the house. Beyond the space for her shop, there lay a kitchen with more cupboards, another fireplace and a brick oven. Upstairs she found a bedroom with a sturdy oak bed and dresser and an ample wardrobe, a sitting room with a comfy chair, and even a small lavatory with a washstand and basin and a brass chamber pot.

All day she unloaded and unpacked her crates of supplies, sorting and arranging some of her potions, ointments, tools, pots, herbs and healing recipes downstairs in her shop. She placed her locked chest of spell books, talismans, amulets and other miscellany in a convenient corner and toted her two trunks of belongings upstairs. After airing out her clothes and arranging them in the wardrobe and in the dresser drawers, she moved her sewing basket to the sitting room. Then she made up her new bed with blankets and pillows, smoothing her mother's quilt on top. The last thing she unpacked that day were her few knickknacks, keepsakes that she placed here and there for a personal touch.

As the sun set, she lit candles, made and ate a light supper from food she brought, then washed and dressed for bed. She locked the door to her new home, shuttered the windows and blew out all but one candle. With that last light showing the way, she climbed the stairs to her bedroom and snuggled under the bed covers. Then she blew out the candle flame and drifted off to sleep, happy.

Stone walls surrounded her. A handsome man stood in front of a stone table. A spell book lay open on the table, and the man was reading from it. The room erupted in a glow...

"Get out!"

Annalisa awoke with a start, the shout from her dream

still ringing in her ears. Her heart pounded and sweat dripped down her cheek, or maybe it was a tear. It had been a long time since she had a vision dream. She thought, hoped, they had stopped. Annalisa sat up, curling her arms around her knees. She stayed like that for a while, before settling back into a restless sleep.

The early morning light found her in better spirits, and she pushed the odd dream to the back of her mind. "It's nothing," she whispered to herself, "just a flicker of the past, probably someone who used to live here." Yet, she knew she always dreamed for a reason.

Her unease faded as the day unfolded and her chores occupied her time. By sunset, she had her shop ready to her satisfaction—enough to open, at any rate—and hung her painted sign over the door. She gave it a last look to make certain it hung straight.

"Perfect. 'Healing and Herbal Remedies.' Now all I need are customers." A task for tomorrow, however. Annalisa settled in for the night, eventually retiring to bed and a dreamless sleep.

The morning greeted her with sunshine. After dressing and a hearty breakfast, she set out to make the most of her day. To that end, she gathered a basket, locked her door and walked down to the hall as Thomas asked. She also wanted to browse the town shops for some provisions and a small bag of oats for Pebble; he couldn't live on the hay she brought with her forever. She hummed as she walked, a pretty tune she learned as a child. Her mood cheerful, she entered the hall and found Thomas.

"I wanted to let you know I have the shop ready."

"Wonderful, splendid. I'll spread the word."

With that done, Annalisa said goodbye, left and wandered down High Street toward the town market quarter. She passed by the shop district on her arrival, so she knew to head back towards the town square. Annalisa walked with a bounce in her step, still humming, revelling in the morning with its clear blue sky and crisp air.

She passed by houses and waved hello to townspeople starting their day, exchanging pleasantries and directions with others on their way to market. Soon she left High

Street, moving onto Market Road and the hustle and flurry of Eastwych's heart. She emerged onto the rows of shops that lined the intersecting streets, painted in bright colours. Decorated signs hung from their doors and eaves to announce their specialty. Some had bright striped awnings, some had tables or stalls standing outside, displaying wares, but all were bustling and busy in the morning sun.

The strong whiff of ale assaulted her as she passed Brewer Street, to mix with the pungent scent of fish when she crossed Fisher Row. Annalisa smiled as she surveyed this hectic world, enchanted by the noise of barkers selling their goods, of haggling customers, the smell of baking bread and fresh butchered meat. The din and aromas filled her senses with joy.

As she walked, she made a note of the wool merchant and weaver, the blacksmith and the tailor for future trips. Annalisa fingered pieces in the jeweller's stall—nodding politely at Emeline as she did—wondering if she should indulge and buy one of the pendants. She especially liked a silver creation in the shape of a dragon with intricate metalwork and inlaid crystal gems. From the corner of her eye, she saw a stern-faced Emeline watching her.

"I don't like dawdlers. If you can't afford to buy, move on." The sudden voice and Emeline's sharp tone snapped her attention away from her musings. Annalisa's mood soured under the metalsmith's withering look, and she withdrew her hand from the display.

"If that's the way you feel, I think I will go." Feeling angry and slighted, she turned her back on Emeline and her jewellery, deciding to spend her money elsewhere.

She felt better when she stopped at the produce merchant, where she purchased some tubers and violet leeks to make a savoury pie. At the butcher's she procured a fresh cut of pig wrapped in paper for her supper and bought some sweet buns from Rose the baker that she tucked in a corner of her basket. Lastly, she added some milk and cheese from the dairy, and on her way back she stopped at the livery. There she arranged the delivery of some oats and feed for Pebble.

As she left the livery, she caught sight of her helpful carpenter, Gregor, the man she met on her first day in town.

He worked shirtless, sawing a piece of lumber outside his shop. Her heart beat a little faster as the muscles rippled in his exposed back. She fiddled with her hair and went to say hello.

"You have some lovely pieces." Annalisa ran her hand over a well-crafted chair he had on display outside his shop.

"Thank you, are—oh, it's you." He smiled at her. "Hello again."

"Um, I'm sorry to bother you when you're working, I mean you were so helpful the other day, I..." Her words dangled in the air, her manner flustered as she stared at Gregor, sweat dripping down his bare chest.

"I don't mind. I could use a rest." He seemed unaware of her discomfiture. "Got settled, did you? Thomas put you up in that vacant place on Red Tree Lane, didn't he?"

Annalisa smiled shyly. "Yes, he did, thank you. I've settled in nicely. My apothecary is ready for business."

"Excellent. I'll pass the word on. You should talk to Elam. He sells spices, herbs and teas, and he'd most likely let you sell ready-made remedies and potions in his shop. He's on Gilded Lane, Tasty Teas and Tidbits."

"I'll do that, thank you." Annalisa fidgeted, her mind spinning for conversation topics. "I'm off then, back to my shop."

"Goodbye. Stop in again if you need anything or want to talk. I'd be happy to show you around town or answer any questions you may have."

"Oh, thank you. I might do that." Annalisa walked away with a bounce in her step and returned to her house, after a quick stop and a word with Elam, where she made arrangements to sell her wares.

The rest of the morning she spent in busy work, tidying and arranging, but around midday she attended to the fishmonger's apprentice, who needed a cut cleaned, stitched and dressed. After a late lunch she served two customers, one wanting some powder to relieve headaches, and the other a cough remedy. She gave the shop a good sweeping after that, and she was putting away the broom as Gregor and an older grey-haired woman wandered inside.

"My aunt Ina is looking for a—"

"I can speak for myself, Gregor." The grim-faced, thin-lipped woman stared at Annalisa. "Not much, but I suppose you'll have to do. I need a ward against curses, young woman, and a charm of luck as well. Can you do that?"

Taken aback, Annalisa blurted, "You think someone wants to cast a curse on you?"

"Oh, they're all plotting against me. I have to be clever, though, and stop them before they spread their evil. Can you help me?"

Annalisa nodded as she bit her lip to keep from smiling. "I have just what you need." She took the key from around her neck and walked to her chest in the corner. She unlocked it, rummaged for a bit and withdrew a two-sided magical amulet with a small charm attached. Then she picked out a hanging talisman and returned to Gregor's aunt.

"These should do the trick. This spelled amulet will reflect any magic back on the caster, plus the added charm gives good fortune to the wearer." Annalisa handed it to Ina, who slipped it around her wrinkly neck.

Then Annalisa held up the talisman. "Hang this over your front door and no evil will ever darken your home."

Ina grabbed the talisman and cackled. "Oooh, they'll not get me now. Pay the girl, Gregor, I'm going home." And with that, she whirled about and walked out of the shop.

Gregor sighed as she left and reached into his money pouch for coin. "How much?"

"Five coppers."

"Reasonable." He handed the payment to Annalisa. "I'm sorry about her, she's batty."

"Not at all. She just has a unique spirit."

"Nice of you to say, but she's an odd one. Wasn't always like that, but these days..." He shrugged, and then winced.

Annalisa noticed at once. "Are you in pain?"

"Nothing much, my shoulder's sore from work."

"Oh, I have something for that." She moved to her shelves and took down a small jar of balm, then went back to Gregor, handing him the medicine. "Rub that on your skin, over where it's sore. It'll help with the pain."

"Thank you. What do I owe you?"

"Take it as a gift. For the help you gave, and your kindness." She smiled.

He smiled back. "Nice of you. Thank you again." He took hold of her hand and squeezed it gently, nodded goodbye and left.

Annalisa's mood soared, the warm touch of his hand making her fingers tingle. Even the fact she had no further customers couldn't dampen her spirits. She crawled into her bed that night still feeling giddy.

She stood outside on a patch of grass, away from Eastwych, looking upward. Not at the night sky—although she could see it with its stars—but at the tower, a tall grey monolith. She recognized it as the structure she had passed on her arrival to town, but it seemed less...neglected. It glowed from the inside, and a shadow flickered through the window.

A figure stood there, the same man from the previous dream; she knew that even though she couldn't see his face. And she knew he was upset, frantic...

"Leave! Just leave!"

Her eyes flashed open and the dream vanished, leaving

her shaking. She shivered under the covers; the room seemed colder. She curled into a ball under her bedclothes and shuddered, a strange dread in her bones. She shut her eyes again, and as they closed, for a heartbeat she thought she saw a fading light shimmer at the edge of the shadows. Sleep didn't come for a long time.

In the morning she climbed out of bed, blurry-eyed and yawning, dressed, ate breakfast and headed out to the market for more supplies. Annalisa felt out of sorts and lethargic as she stopped at the produce stand. She yawned for the third time in as many minutes, her eyes trying to focus on the fresh vegetables arranged in the stall.

"Those tubers boring, are they?" Mereck the grocer smiled at her.

Annalisa giggled. "No, I had a bad night's rest, is all."

"That'd do it, all right. Not much worse than trying to do a day's work after a bad night."

"Annalisa."

She turned to see Gregor, who had a fair-haired young girl trailing after him. She smiled at them both.

"Doing your morning shopping, I see. Stocking up for the Fire Festival? Oh, this is my niece Giselle, by the way." He nodded at the girl.

"Hello, Giselle. Nice to meet you." She held out her hand to the child who looked about eleven or twelve. The girl shook her hand with vigour.

Annalisa turned back to Gregor. "What's the Fire Festival?"

"You don't know about the Fire Festival?" Words tumbled out of Giselle's mouth at a rapid pace. "Oh my, it's the best. Oh, the Fire Festival is magnificent. It happens on the Day of the Long Sun, a few days from now. We decorate the square and have music and dancing. There are booths for food and wares and games, and play-acting where we all wear masks and costumes. Last year Gregor was a juggler and entertained everyone, and I was a spring maiden and wore new green ribbons in my hair. Then at sunset we all take our masks off and have a bonfire and supper." The girl took a deep breath and clapped her hands in excitement.

"Sounds like great fun."

"It is, I love it. It's the best time of the cycle. My uncle says you are a healer, and you have magic. That means you just have to come. You could have a booth with remedies and potions and do your magic for your customers. That would be perfect. You have to come. Say you'll come."

Annalisa grinned, livened by her enthusiasm. "Of course I'll come. I don't know what sort of costume I can create in a few days though."

"Try Raphael's shop. He sells masks and simple costumes this time of year." Gregor nodded towards the wool merchant. "I'll escort you there if you like."

"That would be nice."

The three wandered over to the wool shop, where Giselle insisted on picking out a mask for Annalisa. She chose a blue half-mask embroidered with silver stars, while Annalisa picked out a sleeveless indigo robe to compliment it. The three continued shopping for a spell, and then Gregor escorted Annalisa home without his niece, who ran off to join some friends.

Annalisa took a breath. "Do you mind if I ask you something about this area?"

"Don't know how much help I can be, but go ahead."

"Oh, good." She took a breath to steady herself. "I'm curious about the tower outside of town. What's the history of the place?"

"That eyesore? Used to be some wizard's keep, long time past. His family helped found Eastwych, but this wizard holed up in the tower. A regular hermit, he was, until he vanished."

"He vanished?" Annalisa felt a chill.

"Yep. One day he was there and the next he was gone. Left everything behind too. Never found out why. His family doesn't live here anymore either. Last of them moved away in my father's day. Had some young man of theirs nosing round a few years back though, looking for his roots, he said, and the answer to why that wizard up and disappeared."

"Thank you." Annalisa allowed the matter to drop, partially satisfied, if bewildered as to why she continued to dream of some wizard long gone and most likely dead. As they arrived at her house, she gave Gregor a smile. "Thank you for walking me home. I'll let you get back to your work."

"I enjoyed the walk, I hope to do it again." Gregor smiled back and she blushed. She ducked her head with a mumbled goodbye and hurried inside her shop.

She was inside the tower keep again. The air was hot and hard to breathe. She felt confined and frightened. In front of her, the man—no, the wizard—stood by the stone table with the open spell book. She could hear his voice chanting as he worked an incantation, and she saw a growing sphere of silver light hovering between his outstretched hands. She stared at its energy, mesmerized for a moment. Then she forced her gaze away, her body shaking.

"You shouldn't have come."

Annalisa looked back and saw the wizard gazing at her. His face made her heart ache, so handsome and so very, very sad.

"You have to leave!"

She woke trembling and afraid, still seated in the chair where she had fallen asleep. The fading light outside told her the sun was setting, so she rose, closed her shop and made supper. She went to bed early, and sleep did not come easily to her that night, but thankfully, neither did any dreams.

Several days later, after much hurried preparations and Gregor's generous help, she stood at her booth as part of Eastwych's Fire Festival. Around her the town talked and strolled among the festooned booths and stalls, decorated with ribbons and colourful paint. People laughed and danced as rambling musicians played their stringed instruments and their skin drums, entertaining all with merry tunes. There were jugglers and tumblers, gambolling for the crowds, townsfolk dressed in masks and costumes. Before her spread sprites and elves, kings and queens, mingling and having fun.

Annalisa smiled in her blue mask, feeling regal in her new robe. She answered questions from those who stopped, sold them remedies and worked a bit of magic for their amusement. She did simple tricks: making ribbons float and twirl, creating a small flying dragon of light, disappearing and reappearing coins. Her efforts received applause and smiles, especially from the children.

As the afternoon wore on, she stood chatting with Gregor during a lull in customers.

"Are you enjoying the festivities?" Gregor leaned against her booth.

"Yes, it's great fun, and sales have been brisk. I think—" Her words dangled, unsaid, as a sparkle of radiance caught her attention. A silver glow, unformed and ethereal, quivered a few feet away. As she watched, it took shape, transforming into a form—a man. She heard a voice speaking to her, but she kept her eyes locked on the apparition.

He stood there, dazzling and lustrous in front of her, translucent and glittering, dressed in an iridescent grey robe that flapped around his ankles. He gestured frantically with his hands as Annalisa stared through him to the milling people across the square.

"What do you want?" Her voice escaped her in a whisper, and Gregor responded.

"Who are you talking to, Annalisa?"

"Don't you see him?" Fear crawled under her skin.

"See who?"

Then she knew for certain. A waking vision, the worst manifestation of her power. "No one. I'm talking to no one."

She tried to run away, abandoning her booth, a worried Gregor close behind her, but the vision came with her. He stared at her, this apparition, and Annalisa noticed his eyes. The colour of grey smoke and reflected pain. A small part of her soul understood that pain, and she reached out her hand instinctually with sympathy.

"Why aren't you listening? Why don't you leave? GET OUT!"

The furious roar set Annalisa back on her heels, pierced her unprepared emotional defences and cracked what tiny shred of self-control she still possessed.

"Why don't I leave? Why don't you leave? Leave me alone! Leave me in peace! Stop haunting me with your spells and your dreams and your anger! Go away! Just go away! Get out of my head, you wizard, and go back where you came from!"

The air snapped and sputtered around the spectre and he vanished, leaving Annalisa facing the gaping stares of a crowd of astonished onlookers.

"Oh my, what an outburst." The bewildered voice of

Thomas Madder broke the awkward silence, followed by a chorus of others.

"What happened?"

"Is it a game, a show?"

"Why did she scream like that?"

"Is she sick?"

"I *told* you the girl was odd."

"What's wrong with you?"

Annalisa trembled and squeaked in embarrassment, unable to face the barrage of questions. She fled the square mortified, her face flushed and her confidence broken.

She heard footsteps behind her, but she kept on running all the way to her door. As she fumbled with the lock and key, a hand touched her shoulder.

"What happened, Annalisa?"

Gregor's voice made her crumble inside and she started sobbing. "I didn't mean to cause trouble, but I can't help the visions. I wish I could, but I can't."

Gregor gently took the key from her, opened the front door and led her inside. She sat down in the nearest chair and he knelt beside her. "Tell me."

Annalisa took a breath and wiped her cheeks with the back of her hand. "I have dreams, and sometimes visions. Mostly of things that have happened. It's part of my gift. Magic weaves itself around our world, Gregor, and it leaves remains."

"Remains?"

"Think of it like the sawdust left behind when you work, only unseen, part of the air and the earth. I can sense that leftover magic, and it can give me dreams. Of people and places, events or the history of a place. Usually it fades, as the magic grows weaker. Not this time, it's getting stronger and I don't know why. I keep dreaming of the keep outside of town, and a wizard. He keeps telling me to get out, to leave town. I don't understand why I'm dreaming about him, but I want it to stop."

She sighed. "That's what I saw in the square today. I had a waking vision of this wizard." She ducked her head, avoiding Gregor's eyes. "It's happened before, where a vision occurred in public, worse than today. It was humiliating.

People I thought were my friends treated me differently afterwards. They shunned me for months, people only talking to me if they needed a healer. I finally had to leave." She sighed. "I imagine it will happen here now—the gossip, the whispers behind my back of how strange I am." Her mouth twisted into a bitter smile. "I came here to start fresh, away from the stares. Now I have to face it again."

"Some may act like that, but not everyone will. I won't hold it against you." He put his finger under her chin, lifted her head until their eyes met and kissed her. Then he smiled. "I won't hold it against you at all."

She inhaled, the taste of his lips still warm on her mouth. "Thank you."

For a moment there was intimate silence between them, and then he rose. "I'll leave you be, but I'll come round later to see how you are."

She stared at the door after he left, her emotions in turmoil.

⁘

The next morning found her still feeling humiliated,

despite Gregor's understanding and comfort. The curious and the malicious descended after her outburst the previous day, and she spent the afternoon and evening attempting to answer for her behaviour and evading the judgemental. It hadn't been as bad as she feared, as Gregor helped stave off the worst— and kept a gloating Emeline at bay—but still it had been a trying day. At least the night had been dream free.

When the sun filtered in her window the next morning, she wanted to remain in her bed, but she forced herself up to face another day, and after breakfast she went to the market. No one engaged her in friendly banter as she did her shopping; most folk avoided her presence, and for the ones who didn't, she ducked their pitying gazes. Yet she encountered none of the unpleasantness she feared until she turned a corner at the bakery. Rose and Emeline were chatting for all to hear.

"That Annalisa might have a gift for healing, but she's touched in the head by that magic of hers. That commotion she caused at the festival, going on about wizards, shouting at the air like something was there. Nonsense."

"That's what comes from recruiting outsiders. I warned Thomas, and now we have *her*. That's not the worst part. She's got Gregor believing in her foolishness, the poor besotted fool. I hear he's been asking questions about the keep down the road. Can you imagine? That thing's been abandoned for years…"

The conversation drifted out of earshot as Annalisa hurried past the two women. She kept her composure and her temper, resisting the urge to defend herself and Gregor against their gossip until she put distance between them. Then she paused, her eyes closed, her cheeks flushed in chagrin, before leaving the morning market.

Annalisa travelled less than a street length before she heard footsteps behind her and a voice hailed her.

"Annalisa, wait."

She slowed her steps and allowed Gregor to match his pace to hers.

"I'm not sure what it means, if it has anything to do with those visions of yours, but I thought you should know. About the old keep. Wilhelm's son says he saw a light in the place last eve, around dusk. Said it looked different too, better somehow. Don't know if it's important, could be just a vagrant, or the boy spinning tales, but still...it's odd."

Annalisa shivered, a tremor of anxiety invading her mind. "It's—it's probably nothing, just a coincidence." Her voice didn't sound convincing, even to herself. "You should forget about it, Gregor, forget about my dreams and visions. That's what I plan to do."

"I'm not sure that's wise, Annalisa, this could be important."

She turned to look at him. "Not as important as making a home here. I don't want to be an outsider again, and I don't want you to be one either."

He took her hand in his, squeezing. "I don't care about what the townsfolk think. It's unsettling, there being lights at the keep now, with you having those dreams and such. I'm heading out today to the market at Bromford for some trading. I'll be gone for a few days. Come with me. I don't like you being here alone."

Some voice screamed in the back of her head, *"Go with*

him!" His voice, the wizard's voice, clear in her mind as if he stood whispering in her ear. Part of her shouted, "Listen," but the words that tumbled from her mouth didn't obey, ruled by her insecurities, her resentment and her anger.

"No, no. I won't be chased out, not by you, not by those women, not by anyone. Not again. Never again!"

Gregor dropped her hand. "Fine then." He backed away.

"No, wait." Annalisa grabbed at his arm. "I didn't mean to be so cross, it's just..." She let the sentence trail off, unable to explain. "I can't go today, is all. I have to deliver the medicine for Mrs. Durville's cough and tend to Mr. Chauncey. His dressing needs changing." She turned her head away from Gregor's anxious eyes. "Besides, how would it look, me running off with you. Why, it would set tongues wagging, and I have enough of that already." The disapproval of those women, the town, her past, still clung to her and she shut everything else out.

Gregor sighed, regret etched in his voice. "I'm sorry, but I understand. If you change your mind, I don't leave until noon."

He walked away, leaving Annalisa feeling suddenly lost and alone.

She spent the rest of the day as planned, her decision not to leave with Gregor weighing on her thoughts. The voice kept whispering in her head, *"go, go, go,"* until she climbed into bed that night and slipped into an uneasy sleep.

She stood at the centre of a whirlwind, the air both icy and blistering, a wail filling her ears. Around her the walls of the keep shook, stone fragments tumbling. Through a hoary fog of sparks, she saw the wizard screaming as the surrounding space burned, crackled, popped, alight in a turbulent silver radiance. Annalisa knew what she saw was magic, a feral spell, out of control and devouring the wizard with its power. She tried to scream, but no sound uttered from her mouth. She could only watch her wizard writhe in agony.

Somehow, through his obvious pain, he turned and looked at her.

"Why didn't you leave? Now it's too late."

Annalisa woke shrieking. Her bedroom wasn't dark, as

if moonlight bathed it in its luminosity. But there was no moon. Beside her bed, stood the shade of the wizard, the one who tried to warn her. Through the window Annalisa saw what caused the glow, the sky ablaze in the same colour as the light in her dream. She turned to her apparition with fear in her eyes. She understood.

"A time displacement spell went wrong." Her voice trembled. "Past events are about to collide with us."

"Yes." He reached out in a futile gesture. "I'm sorry. I tried to stop it, but I could only delay the inevitable."

Annalisa could do nothing as magic engulfed the village.

Gregor returned along the road to Eastwych a few days later, glad to be headed back home. His wagon clattered, laden with traded goods, and his pouch jingled, filled with coin from his sales. He sang a snippet from his favourite song and smiled at the thought of seeing Annalisa again. His previous worries were long gone.

The stench of charred wood and smoke gave him the first indication of trouble, then he saw the wreckage of the old tower. Chunks of cauterized stone littered the land, strewn across black and baked ground and among burnt trees. The sight of the former keep made his stomach churn. He snapped the reins and hastened the pace of his horse and wagon. He charged through a blistered landscape, scarred in seared vegetation and heavily dotted with scorched and broken woodland. Panic rose in his throat like bile; he had to reach his home. He raced down the road, wagon wheels spinning dust and cinders, veering wildly around the curves, speeding to Eastwych.

Then a new smell hit him, something putrid and tinged with burnt metal and smoke. When he neared the town, he yanked on the reins, skidding the wagon to a stop in a spray of dirt and soot. He stared in horror at the devastation that had once been Eastwych.

Gregor scrambled down from his wagon, staggered a few steps, and collapsed to his knees, numb and shocked. He despaired at the sight, a scream bubbling down deep, his cheeks wet with tears. Before him, stretched out in a ravaged vista, lay blackened and consumed ruins, not the town he knew and loved. Nothing was left, nothing but rubble, ashes, and bones for as far as he could see.

And somewhere in the distance he heard a voice whisper, "I'm sorry."

When Gods Roar

The late morning air shattered with a deafening bellow, a thunderous primeval screech. The window glass shook, the shutters vibrated, and the sky exploded in radiance.

The Pantheon were hunting again.

Bent over the porcelain basin full of soapy water and half-dirty dishes, Elenora shuddered, deep memories stirred by the cacophony assailing her ears. She paused, staring out the kitchen window, longing filling her heart. Their haunting call screamed to her soul, as it aroused the deep-buried essence of her bestial nature. Her fingers trembled as she looked back to her chores and submerged her hands in the water to wash the breakfast dishes.

Why am I here? I want to be back there with them. My gods, my masters. I was happy then.

Elenora missed the sharp, bitter wind on her skin, the earthy smell of the forest, the nights sleeping at her masters' feet as the bonfires raged. She missed the hunt, the wind in her face, the thrill as she closed in on her prey. Most of all she missed the power of her masters and their raw magnificence. Nothing within this insignificant house compared.

Elenora closed her eyes and listened to their sweet voices. How she longed to run again as a Hound of the Gods. To hear their booming voices, to smell the blood from a fresh kill or feast on their scraps. Oh, to bask in their glory again, to feel one of their infrequent and indifferent caresses. She had lived in their magnificent shadow, and it had been enough. More than enough, it had been everything.

"Take me back." The raucous echo in the air swallowed her quiet whisper. "Take me home."

A tear dripped from her cheek and hit the soapy water. The children's laughter echoed from the next room. She turned her head, but no one was watching.

Good. They wouldn't understand. None of them understand.

She hated the men who stole her away—the Cabal, they called themselves. She took a wrong turn that night, and the hunter became hunted. Their magic users brought her down, stole everything that made her special, and transformed her from hound to human.

"They saved me, they said." Her murmurs surged out bitter. "Proclaimed me free from my slavery to the gods. But they only traded me into another form of slavery: marriage." She spat into the dishwater. "They gave me no say in a husband and wed me to a widower I did not love. Saddled me with two children not of my blood."

Her thoughts flickered on her husband. A kind man, but she still had little feeling for him. All her love remained with the Pantheon. Had she remained, she would have mated with another Hound and had children of her own to serve the gods. Now, that life was dead.

A squeak of a hinge and a thumping inside the doorway told her that same husband returned from his chores. A cheery whistling followed. She sighed and tore her thoughts away from her dreams. She listened to his voice greet the children.

He'll be looking for me next. Why couldn't he stay outside?

Elenora gave another sigh and looked down at the dishes. She resisted the urge to smash them to the floor.

Driven indoors by the gods, no doubt. They fear them so. They can't see their magnificence.

She tensed as she heard footsteps approach.

"Elenora."

She closed her fingers in a fist. She knew what was coming.

He placed a gentle hand on her shoulder. She managed not to shudder. He kissed her cheek. She nearly winced. His touch reminded her of what she lost.

"We should all stay inside today. It's not safe."

Not safe for whom? You perhaps. For those whelps I never wanted, certainly. But I want to be out there. I want to be in the shadow of my gods.

She nodded. "Of course. Whatever you think best."

⁙

She tried to hide her true self, caught in this trap with

no way of escape. Stolen from the gods, she had nowhere to run; her masters would not accept back a tainted Hound. Not without an offering. She had seen a few try to return. None had succeeded.

So Elenora suffered, existing as her longing ate away at her thoughts, and the days flowed into each other. Outwardly she smiled at her husband and children; she allowed him to touch her, allowed herself to feed and care for her family. Repeat the routine to stave off the madness.

Most days she fed her yearning with remembrance. The grit of loam and decaying leaves beneath her fingers, the charred taste of cooked meat ripped from the bone by her teeth. On the bad days she daydreamed. Envisioned herself taking a knife and eviscerating her family while they slept. On those days she missed the scent of blood in her nostrils, the putrid tang of spilled entrails, the dead look in the eyes of the newly killed prey. Those days were the hardest to bear.

Eventually her husband noticed and called the Cabal elders. He sat her down one day as three stern men entered her home. The men looked at her with undisguised disgust, before turning to her husband.

"Do you condemn your wife as unrepentant?"

Elenora scowled as her husband nodded and replied, "I do."

In the next instant, the three men grabbed her and forced her outside, dragging her screaming from her house. They threw her to the ground.

Elenora stared at them, and spat. She noticed her husband remained in the house.

Coward. Not brave enough to witness what he's done.

The three Cabal elders circled her and pronounced judgement.

"Elenora Noveer, you have been accused and found guilty on evidence of your lawful husband. You still embrace the false gods, refuse the grace of reclamation, the grace of liberation from evil. You must let go of the last vestiges of your tainted transgressions and embrace the true path denied to you for so long. Will you renounce the Pantheon?"

She turned her face away and did not answer. Once, she would have cut them, torn them limb from limb, but no more. The Cabal stripped the blood of the gods from her veins and left her with only the memories. These men turned her powerless and laid her at their mercy. She could not give them what they wanted.

"We ask again. Do you denounce the Pantheon and their barbaric ways? Do you accept the human path?"

Elenora hung her head and stayed silent. She feared what would come next, but she could not lie. Not about that.

The elders sighed. "Very well. We will cleanse you. We will beat the evil out. Your stubborn will must be shattered and reformed. We must save you, Elenora."

The men dragged her to the front fence, to the stocks that were part of every Cabal member's home. Once locked in, unable to fight back, she heard the slither of the leather whip being uncoiled and braced for the lashes. They came fast and hard, the thwacking, slashing sting across her back, cutting through her dress and into skin. The smell of her own blood fed her memories and strengthened her resolve; she would not give in. She counted ten, fifteen, and then more lashes until she lost count, until she screamed in pain, until she bordered on unconsciousness from the fiery agony searing across her back. Her knees buckled and she hung from the stocks, dangling like meat. Only then did they stop beating her.

Elenora swayed, the world fading in and out, but she heard one of the elders whisper, "I remember you from your reclamation. You resisted then as well. Days we beat you before you submitted to our will, before you returned to the right path. Let go of the evil you cling to, let go of the Pantheon. Submit to the Cabal, submit to your husband. Accept your human existence."

Elenora finally nodded, unable to suffer any more, willing to do anything to be rid of the Cabal Elders. The man backed away. Elenora's husband stepped forward, stroking her hair. She wanted to gag but suppressed the reflex. Then she heard the voice of the elder.

"She will stay in the stocks for two more hours. Then you may tend to her. If she continues to resist us, we will return and repeat the cleansing."

Elenora closed her eyes as footsteps retreated from her. Silence settled and she knew peace. She breathed in the smell of the trees and the scent of her own blood. She dreamed of running with her gods.

Elenora behaved more circumspect after she recovered, careful to keep her true thoughts hidden behind false smiles and cheery words. Her husband seemed satisfied, and the Cabal Elders did not return.

Yet, when alone, she sometimes stared at the forest edge in the distance, her heart breaking. At night she dreamed of the smell of pine and the dark looming shadows beyond the fire. Every day her desperate dream faded, and resignation to her fate settled over her like a shroud. Day by day she moved through the world a ghost of who she was, until the days turned to months and the first bite of winter came with the frost.

That day the clouds gathered, yet her husband seemed cheerful as he returned from an early morning meeting with the Cabal.

"Good news. There has been a raid. We've dealt a great blow to the false gods. The Cabal plans a celebration on the morrow. We shall attend."

Elenora suppressed a shudder and held back the tears.

She would pretend, but her heart would not celebrate. The children ran into the room and tugged at her skirts.

"You promised us cookies, Mama."

She looked at them with no smile, but she was glad of the distraction from her husband's news. "So I did. Come to the kitchen." She led them away, leaving her husband behind. She sat them down at the table and fed them each a cookie.

Shouts snapped the quiet, and an unearthly rumble shook the house. Elenora grabbed the cupboard to steady herself, and the children cried out through mouthfuls of crumbs. A deep, vibrant bellow thundered from outside, "Bring out the humans!"

The front door burst open and swarms of leather-clad men rushed inside, hauling Elenora and the children outdoors. She heard a struggle from inside, and then witnessed her husband dragged out, sporting a bloody nose and face. The men dumped him beside the frightened and whimpering children.

But none of that held Elenora's attention past a glance. No, her focus was on the behemoth that filled the space beyond the garden. She stared in rapture at the creature that towered far above the trees, its many eyes reflecting the colour of the sky and its appendages spread out over the grass and road. Half the fence and the dreaded stocks lay crushed under the weight of one of those tentacles. Two of her husband's sheep crunched between its teeth.

She whispered its name, "Rylthu."

Rylthu cast his gaze at her. "How do you know my name?"

Elenora trembled. "I served as your Hound. I hunted prey for you until the Cabal ripped me from your arms."

Rylthu gnashed his teeth. "An outcast Hound? Here? Fitting, perhaps. Did you leave of your own accord, or were you taken by the vile Cabal?"

"I was taken."

"Rescued, you mean!" Her husband's angry voice shouted from behind her. "As will all Hounds some day!" He scowled. "I know why you are here, abomination, but you have no power over us! The treaty forbids it! This land is not in your territory!"

"Do not speak of treaties! The Cabal does not abide

by treaties! Not after today. They have destroyed a nest! A nest! The stealing of Hounds, we overlooked, but this will not go unanswered!"

Elenora shivered, tears forming in her eyes. A nest destroyed? The children of the gods killed? Unthinkable.

She took a step forward, addressing Rylthu. "Do you seek revenge, Great One? I know well the evil of the Cabal and share your hatred. I will tell you everything I know and help you take your vengeance, if that is what you wish." Elenora inhaled and dared everything with her next words. "All I ask in return is to be your Hound again." She dropped to her knees and begged, "Please, let me come back. Let me serve again!"

Rylthu whirled his eyes and his voice boomed, "Yes, we seek revenge. Such an offer is interesting." A tentacle scraped the ground. "Yet impossible. You are culled. Our blood has been removed from your body. You are a tainted thing now. How can we take such as you back? Even for this?"

"I never wanted to be culled!" Elenora's voice rose in pitch, nearly hysterical. She could taste her happiness. She would not lose it again. "The Cabal stole me from you! I will give them to you gladly. I was never less than yours. Never wanted to leave! Take me back, I beseech you!"

Rylthu growled. "What you say is true. The Cabal takes many Hounds. Yet…what about these puny mortals? The ones that tie you here?" An appendage waved at her family. "This mate and these mewling whelps."

She turned and stared at her family. Her husband stared at her, appalled, his arms wrapped around his children. In that instant she knew hatred and the words tumbled out.

"I care nothing for them! Take them!" Her heart leapt at the idea, and her voice filled with joy. "My husband is Cabal. Let him be your first act of vengeance. Take them as my offering, my gift for restoration into your service."

She heard her husband cry out in protest but paid him no heed.

"You would give them as an offering? Proof of your faith?" The resonance from Rylthu's voice shook the air.

"Yes, yes!" Her voice dripped in eagerness. "I give them willingly. Just take me back!"

"Elenora, no! What are you saying?" Her husband reached out to her, but it was too late. Rylthu snaked an elongated limb around her family and dragged them into his voracious grasp. Then the beast looked down at her.

"Are you certain?"

Ignoring the shouts and pleas of her husband and the screams of the terrified children, she shouted, "Yes! A thousand times, yes!"

Rylthu reached out a tentacle and stroked her face. "We accept the offering. You may return to us."

Elenora fell to her knees, euphoric. She tore at her clothes, ripping away the last vestiges of her false life, and bent her naked body in supplication before her god. She vowed, "I am yours, always."

Rylthu laughed and signalled two human followers forward. The dour, weathered men brought her new clothing, led her aside, and dressed her in the customary leathers of her master. She trembled at the feel and smell of the familiar garments and relished the snug fit of the animal skins on her body. She sighed in pleasure as the collar of a Hound tightened around her neck.

Oh, how I missed this.

Elenora raised her head to behold her master.

"Are you ready?"

She nodded.

The beast raised another appendage to his maw and bit; thick, black fluid seeped from the wound. He dangled the dripping tentacle over Elenora's mouth. She opened her lips and accepted the offering of her god. The blood burned as she swallowed, but its magic infused her with power.

I am whole again! I am a Hound of the Gods!

Behind her she heard the screams of her husband and children, and the gnashing of teeth. She inhaled the smell of their blood as Rylthu feasted on their flesh and bones but didn't spare them a care or reflection. Her mind thought only of serving her god and their vengeance on the Cabal.

Gears of the Undead

The church spires cast shadows next to the moon while the gas lamps of the adjoining street flickered in time to the sound of the shovels hitting dirt.

"She'd better pay what she promised, Harry. I don't like this idea of grave robbing. Not without being paid what she promised."

"Shut it, Eddie. She'll pay. Now put your back into the work and clamp down your yapping."

"Don't you complain about my work none," Eddie hissed at his cohort and slammed his spade into the ground, heaving up a mound of earth. "I still don't like it. We're in the middle of bloody London, behind a church. Digging up bodies for a lunatic." He spat, the spittle sliding into the upturned loam. "What if we get caught? It'll be our heads on the block, not hers."

"She's not a lunatic, she's a—a..." Harry fumbled for a minute, rolling the correct word on his tongue. "A *visionary*, that's what she is. A scientist who's looking forward into the years ahead." He smiled like a smug cat with a belly full of cream. "And we won't get caught. Not unless you keep yelping loud enough to wake the dead." Suddenly aware of what he said, Harry clapped a hand across his mouth.

"Don't say that." Eddie shivered and glanced fearfully over his shoulder. "We're in a bloody graveyard, disturbing the dead. Don't summon spirits, Harry, whatever you bloody well do."

"Sorry." Harry ducked his head and continued digging. Under his breath he mumbled a prayer. As he ended with a half-whispered *amen*, his shovel clunked, echoing off wood.

"Hallelujah!" Harry exclaimed, his mood lightening. "That'll be the coffin."

"Good. Let's get this thing out of the ground and delivered."

Pulling their neckerchiefs over their noses to block the stench of death, Harry and Eddie went to work with renewed vigour, unearthing one end of the coffin with all haste. Then, with grunts and a few choice curses, they broke through the wood, wrapped a rope around the body, and hauled the corpse from its final resting place. They loaded the grisly burden onto their wagon and covered it well with a piece of canvas. They filled in the grave, and were soon on their way into the London night, with no one the wiser for their misdeed.

The horses' hooves clomped down the cobblestone streets in a soothing rhythm, the rattles and creaks of the wagon keeping discordant time. Eddie cast surreptitious glances every few feet, still nervous and looking for police.

"What if the peelers stop us, Harry? How will we explain?"

"Stop with the fidgets, Eddie!" Harry hissed, his friend's whining grating on his own nerves. "It ain't like you're an angel. You've done plenty worse than this, and ain't blinked an eye. Why are you going squeamish on me for this job?"

"It's the *nature* of the thing, Harry. Even for me, this

ain't proper, don't feel right. The dead should stay buried. If I didn't need the money so bad…" Eddie sighed. "You're sure she'll pay?"

Harry smiled. "She'll pay."

And with that statement, he flicked the reins and picked up the pace a bit.

⁘

A row of seven gurneys lined the length of the outer wall. Each supported an amalgam of body parts cobbled together with mechanical apparatus and sustained by clanking medical equipment that hissed steam. Doctor Louise Killbride stood over one of her creations—a man strapped down and immobile—adjusting a joint with a spanner and a screwdriver.

"There that should fix your problem. That arm will work in no time, you'll see." She patted the dead flesh of the elbow. "I'll make everything better, don't you worry."

At the sound of her voice, the creature on the metal table turned his head, and his one mechanical eye blinked with a whizz and a click. The other eye did nothing as it was simply an empty socket.

"Wwwhh—wwhhy?" A rasp of guttural sound, of stammered syllables, barely distinguishable as a voice, spewed from his throat. "Wwhhy thhhisss? Ppp—painnn. Tttt—torr—torture." The last word sounded clear as a Sunday church bell and caught Doctor Killbride by surprise.

"It's not torture." She smiled and smoothed the little remaining hair on his head, as one would a frightened child. "It's rebirth. And like all birth it's painful and confusing. But you mustn't fight it so. Let it happen. And soon we'll all be part of a family." She waved her hand, indicating the other figures arrayed against the wall. "Then we won't feel alone. We'll all be happy. Together. Then you will all understand what I've accomplished. What I've created." She kissed the decayed flesh of his forehead, as a pitiful moan escaped his mouth. Doctor Killbride ignored the soft lamentation. Instead she gave her creation another smile, and repeated, "Soon we'll be a family. All of us. A happy family."

The sound of scuffling feet and grunting drew her attention. Harry poked his head into the laboratory room.

"Where do you want this latest one, Doctor? We drug

him into the corridor here, but we ain't taking him farther till we knows where we're going."

"Put him in cold storage. I made room this morning."

"Will do." Harry disappeared and she heard more grunts and footsteps until they faded away.

"Excellent. Did you hear that, my sweet? Another specimen. Soon I'll be done, with plenty of spare parts, and everything will be perfection."

Another moan came from her creature, but she only laughed, thrilled with the progress of her work.

"What do you think she plans to do with all of 'em? I mean when she's finished remaking the lot of these poor buggers." Eddie asked the question between grunts as they positioned their most recent corpse in the cold storage room among the other dead. "Is she raising an army or sumthin'?"

"Nah!" Harry gave their body one last shove and then wiped the sweat from his brow. "At least I don't think so. She keeps rambling on about family. I think she's just lonely."

"A funny way to go about getting a family. 'Sides, I'd of

thought you'd want live people as family. I'd think it'd be a bit awkward at the holiday dinners with dead people around the table. What d'you feed them?"

"Maybe you wouldn't. Feed them, I mean. Sure cut down on the bills, it would."

"I could use a few less of those." Eddie smirked, and then exclaimed, "Hey, maybe we could give her a bill collector next time. Maybe even a fresh kill." Eddie's smirk turned to a wicked grin.

"Much as I'd like that, she wouldn't. No killing, she said." Harry gave Eddie a stern look. "Anyways, she always sends out for specific sorts. She's particular who we dig up."

"Shame, that bit. There's one of two blokes I wouldn't mind ending and giving over to her."

"I know what you mean. It's tempting, but don't think I'd like crossing the good doctor."

"I suppose. She is, well...the whole thing seems peculiar." Eddie shrugged.

Harry bit his lip and nodded, knowing what Eddie meant but unwilling to label his employer as crazy. At least out loud. "We're better off not questioning, I think."

"Perhaps, but still. The whole thing don't make sense. Why does she do it? And better yet, *how* does she do it? I mean, one of those things of hers is moving, talking. It's not just some barmy scientist messing with corpses and whatnot. She brought a dead person back to life. That ain't natural. That ain't no science I ever heard of, not that I've heard of much, mind, but it fair gives me the willies. What if she's messing with something supernatural or devil worship, or something?"

"I don't know, Eddie, I don't know. That worries me too, how she does it. It ain't natural. But I don't think it's something evil either. But that ain't the thing that worries me the most. It's whether she can control those things of hers."

Eddie whistled in surprise, as if the thought had never occurred to him. "What have we got ourselves into, Harry?"

"I don't know, a mess maybe. I just think of the money and hope things turn out all right. And keep my mouth shut. You should do the same."

"Yeah. I guess we're in too deep now."

Doctor Killbride listened to Harry and Eddie leave, their work finished, and the great clank of the front door slam behind them. She went out and slid home the bolt, locking herself in for the remainder of the night. She wandered back into her operating theatre, facing her creations.

"Hello, my dears. Our friends have left for the night, and we're alone. Time to get to work." A little moan came from the left. "Not you, my sweet. Tonight I'll work on the girls. They're almost ready." She smiled. "I have to attach their new arms and give them another dose of the serum. It will work better on them, with the limited decay. Like it did on you. They should last quite a while before I must replace flesh again." She sighed. "Not like the others." She glanced at the tables farthest from the door. "I waited too long with them. They'll be more machine than flesh by the time I awaken them." Then she turned and flashed a smile at her conscious creation. "Oh well. They'll still be family. Mechanical or not."

She hummed as she walked to the gurneys containing

the strapped down, unconscious bodies of two young girls missing their arms. On a nearby table lay two pairs of clockwork mechanical arms and several syringes. Doctor Killbride picked up one limb and glanced back at the man.

"How old were they when they died? Aged ten and twelve?" The man refused to answer, turning his head. "I suppose it doesn't matter, they're past aging now. But soon you'll be reunited. Won't that be jolly?"

She grabbed a syringe and turned her attention to the girl nearest to her. She injected the syringe's contents into the child's neck and then waited. The girl's eyes flickered and Doctor Killbride smiled.

"Excellent, she's waking up. I can begin."

The doctor fitted the mechanical arm to the child's right stump, ratcheting and securing the metal apparatus in place. She retrieved a screwdriver from the table and one by one tightened the attaching screws through the flesh into bone. The girl's screams filled the room, and she heaved against her restraints as each screw pierced her and fastened her new arm into place. The man's sobbing moans echoed each shriek of the child. Doctor Killbride ignored it all, focusing only on her work until she fused the new arm to the stump.

"There, all done. Now on to the next limb."

The child renewed her shrieks, tears soaking into the gurney's linens, the medical bed creaking under the force of her struggles to escape. Doctor Killbride began to sing a lullaby and scooped up the child's other arm. Then she repeated the procedure for the girl's left arm. At the end, the child subsided into weeping and whimpers. Doctor Killbride injected another syringe of serum into the girl's neck.

She turned to the man. "There now. Your daughter is as good as new. One restored, one to go." She smiled, lifted a remaining clockwork arm and a syringe, and walked to the other child's bed. As she injected the second girl, the man howled his rage and the first child screamed.

Doctor Killbride greeted Harry and Eddie as they entered the foyer of her building. They pulled up short, their chatter at an end, surprised to see their employer.

"Sumthin' wrong, guv?" Harry ventured, afraid of

employment termination.

"Not at all. Just came to wish you two a good morning. I made some tea. Would you care for a cup?"

"Free eats?" Eddie smacked his lips. "Would I ever!"

Harry also nodded his enthusiasm, his worries eased.

"Excellent. Come along to the kitchen, then."

Eddie and Harry exchanged a look that said, "*There's a kitchen?*" but trailed along after Doctor Killbride. They hunkered down at a small wooden table set for three and laden with a tea set, sandwiches and pastries. The doctor poured three cups of tea and joined them. They ate in a rather awkward silence until they devoured most of the food.

"I know the pair of you have been having doubts. About helping me."

Harry and Eddie exchanged guilty looks as they finished the last of their tea. Harry blustered, "Now I don't—"

Doctor Killbride interrupted with a motion of her hand and a stern, "I heard your conversations in the cold storage. The ventilation shaft carries sound quite well." She smiled. "But don't fret. I understand. You just need better motivation." She rose from her chair. "Follow me." She walked from the kitchen with a beckoning glance over her shoulder. The pair shrugged but did as she asked.

Doctor Killbride led them to her laboratory. "You see, this is all very personal to me. Each one of my creations is oh so special." She strolled over to stand beside her first success. The man stared at her with pleading eyes. Doctor Killbride stroked his hair, and her voice softened.

"This was the man I loved. Whom I still love, despite his betrayal. I thought he returned that love, but he lied to me." She moved to her female creature, placing a hand on her arm. The former woman looked terrified. "No, he loved her. His wife. And his daughters." Doctor Killbride nodded at the clockwork hybrid girls on the next two tables. Then she turned back to Harry and Eddie.

"I went a bit mad when I found out he was married. I killed them all. The police never suspected. Not for any of them." She waved her hand at the other three tables of reanimated corpses. "Here lies my stepmother, my shrewish sister and my martinet of a father." She giggled. "Every time

I murdered someone, I thought they would catch me, but they never did."

"Nah." Harry's trembling voice warbled his disbelief. "You didn't. You couldn't. You couldn't have killed all those people."

"Oh, but I did. The guilt, though, it haunted me. It was my remorse that led to my research. So I could fix my mistakes. And I did. Now we can all live happily. As a family."

Harry and Eddie stared at her.

Eddie backed away, looking to run. "You're barmy! I'm gone from this madhouse, I am!"

"No, dear Eddie, you're here to stay. Harry as well." Doctor Killbride giggled again. "I'm bringing you into the family. I put poison in the tea I served you."

Harry and Eddie bolted. They didn't get far. Pain ripped through their guts and they collapsed in the corridors outside the laboratory.

Doctor Killbride knelt beside them, caressing their cheeks as they moaned. "It won't be much longer, and then I can begin. The revival process will be quicker and smoother with such fresh corpses. You should even retain your memories as well, not like some of the older bodies. Poor Father. Not much left in his brain." She smiled a beaming ray of twisted sunshine. "We'll be a family soon. Won't that be ever so lovely?"

The Cold, Dark Heart of the Forest

It peered into the shroud of night, its yellow eyes staring through an infinity of inky black. It discerned shadows and silhouettes—cast by the hinterland forest—fluttering against a blanketing cover of winter. The wind blew across its back, but it felt no cold.

It smiled and slavered its jaws, and fetid breath puffed chalky vapour. With every gnash of its bloody, jagged teeth, wheezing pants kept rhythm with a growling stomach. It shifted position, crouched on its skeletal thin haunches and sniffed the air. The *other* was here as well, in the wind.

"Yes, I am here. The cycle begins again."

It thrashed its head and scrabbled at the snowy

ground. An eager growl rumbled in the back of its throat. *Time to hunt…*

The wind nibbled at her skin, bitter and frosty, even through her parka and scarf. Olivia wanted to be back in the tent, relatively warm, and asleep. Or better yet, at home drinking beer and watching the hockey game. Not traipsing through the north Canadian woods on a winter night because her partner "heard something" and needed to check on the equipment.

Of course, it was her own fault. She volunteered to emulate a popsicle while babysitting climate monitors. She knew the environmental research project was important, but still…

Olivia shook her head. Too late for wishes. The flashlight beam wavered as she stomped her feet and rubbed her gloved hands together. "Are you finished, yet? I'm freezing my butt off, Noah!"

"Just a minute."

The echo of his voice drifted, mixing with the swish of

the breeze tickling the ice in the treetops.

"Yeah, they're fine. We're good, Liv."

"Great. I told you we had nothing to worry about."

In the flashlight's glow she watched Noah's dim outline as he straightened and then saw his familiar smile as he turned to her.

"Better safe than sorry."

"Please. It's just you obsessing. Now, if you're done with your paranoia over the sensors, can we get our butts back in the tent? Before icicles start forming in the wrong places!"

"I'm sure I could find ways to warm you up." Noah smirked suggestively into the flashlight beam.

"In your dreams. Now come on!"

Noah chuckled as he joined her, and they started the trudge back to their camp.

"You know, I don't know why I put up with you." Olivia gave him a friendly nudge.

"Because you secretly love me, that's why."

Olivia huffed and laughed. Inside she cringed, the casual remark hitting closer to home than she cared to admit. She peeked at Noah in a sideways glance, but his attention had turned to the sky.

Noah slowed his pace. "Hey, is it getting lighter?"

"Yeah. I think it is." The beam of Olivia's flashlight grew dim, barely noticeable. "What the—"

The night erupted into brilliance. Streamers of emerald light tinged in violet illuminated the ebon sky, streaking upward in circular sheets of ghostly radiance. The painted luminosity danced, a writhing, waltzing spectacle of fiery electric particles.

"The northern lights!" A shout of glee came from Noah. "I don't believe it!"

Olivia didn't speak as she gazed upward in awe. A tiny cold snowflake landed on her nose, and then another, as a light snowfall descended from the glowing heavens. Olivia stuck out her tongue, as she had when she was a girl. She giggled.

"This is great!" Noah whirled around, doing a lopsided jig. "I've always dreamed of seeing them."

"I know." Olivia rolled her eyes. "One of your *many* obsessions."

"Oh, come on. I'm not that bad."

"Really? For a scientist sometimes you're a bit of a flake. Your ramblings include the northern lights, black holes, parallel universe theory, native mythology, cryptozoology, alien life—"

"Okay, okay, you made your point. I have a lot of freaky interests. You gotta admit it though, the aurora is cool. Look at it."

"Yeah, it's so lovely. Once in a lifetime."

"That's right! We have to record this! Come on, we have to get back to camp! Get the camera! Take some pictures! Video!"

Olivia snapped into research mode as Noah grabbed her arm. "Right. We should document this for—what the blazes! Noah, where's the path?! It's gone!"

"Huh? What do you mean? It's right over…" His words trailed off into the falling snow. A sheen of translucent light barred the way forward. A gleaming, shimmering curtain of energy snaked through the trees blocking their path.

"What the—! *What is that?*" Noah stood motionless, his mouth agape.

"I don't know." Olivia heard the trace of fear in her own whisper. "I've seen nothing like that before. Maybe an electromagnetic phenomenon?"

Noah turned to her and grinned. She saw he was loving this. "Maybe it's aliens." He wiggled his eyebrows in that annoying way she hated. "Or a parallel universe."

"Stop it! Be serious. What are we going to do about this? How are we going to get past it, back to camp?"

"Always so practical. Loosen up. Why would you want to go back to camp? This is an adventure. An undocumented phenomenon. Look at it." Noah waved his hand and tilted his head towards the spectacle, staring. His body shuddered. "Look at it." His voice softened, almost a monotone. "It's beautiful."

A prickle ran down Olivia's neck. "Noah? You okay?"

He didn't answer her question but kept staring. He reminded Olivia of a statue.

"It's so beautiful." He moved a few steps forward. "So beautiful. So beautiful." His voice drifted, taking on a dreamy tone. "Pulsing, shifting. It's like it's calling to us." He took another step forward. "Can you hear it, Liv? Like a melody in light. A siren's song."

"Noah, what are you babbling? Noah?"

Noah ignored her and scuttled forward, getting closer to the phenomenon. "It's waiting, Liv. Waiting for us." His fingers reached out until they were only centimetres away from the barrier.

"Stop! Be careful!" Olivia rushed forward and jerked him backwards. "It could be dangerous!"

He stared at her for a moment, his eyes glazed. He dropped his arm to his side. Then he shook his head and mumbled, "Yeah, I guess." But he didn't move away. He continued to gawk at the energy. "I've seen nothing like it. Is it plasma discharge? Electromagnetic energy from the aurora? Some new anomaly?"

"It's freaking me out, that's what." Olivia tugged at his arm. "Plus, I'm freezing. I say we try to find a way around and leave the thing alone."

"What? No! We need to study it. We can't leave it! We can't!" Noah began to pace. Right and then left, his eyes tracking the radiance. "Come on, Olivia," he coaxed, "this could make our careers."

Olivia shivered. "Noah, you're sounding a little nuts. Obsessive nuts. Okay, maybe we should study it, but how?" Her impatience leached into her voice. "Our equipment is back in the tent, and that—that *thing* is blocking access to the camp. Unless you want to redeploy one of your precious sensors to take some readings?"

Noah ignored her, his attention fixed on the wavering light. "It's right in front of us, Liv, so beautiful. So perfect. Look at it." His body swayed and his foot slid forward on the snow. "It's the aurora, I know it is. Right here, waiting for us, calling." A mellow, almost reverent tone sheathed his words. He moved a step closer.

"That's impossible! The aurora isn't manifesting itself into, whatever this is—Noah!" Olivia shrieked as he lurched forward straight at the wall of scintillation. She reached out, grabbed the sleeve of his coat and immediately felt yanked. She tumbled forward, chasing Noah into the light.

⁂

Olivia shivered, and her head felt as if it spun on a merry-go-round. Cold seeped into her bones and she realized she was face down in the snow, limbs splayed out. She sat up with a dizzy groan, her back and hips twinging. Noah was on all fours to her left, shaking his head.

"What happened, Liv?"

"You tell me. You're the reckless nut job that charged headfirst into that *thing*. You always do that, act without thinking. Why can't you just think first!"

"Hey! Not fair!" Noah threw her his pouty face, the one she hated. "I really don't know what happened. I remember seeing…and feeling… It's all sort of fuzzy."

"*Well*, isn't that convenient? You've maybe dragged us into I don't know what kind of mess, and you don't remember why. At least it's a new variation on getting us into trouble."

"Stop it, Liv. I don't want to argue. My head hurts and this isn't the time."

"It never is." Olivia frowned. "Hey, wait. Where is it? Where's the energy thing?" She craned her neck, trying to find the phenomenon, but it had disappeared. "It's gone."

"What! Oh no."

"See, there you go again. Good riddance if you ask me.

Now we can get back to camp." She noticed something missing. "Do you see the flashlight anywhere?"

Noah shook his head. "We don't need it anyway. The aurora's still lighting up the sky. That'll show us the way back."

"I guess." Olivia frowned again. "Which way is camp? I think I'm all turned around."

"It's that—no, it's—I'm not sure either. Just a sec." He dug into his pocket and smiled. "I still have it!" He pulled out a compass with a flourish. "I'll get our bearing and we'll be all set." Noah frowned. "Um. Something's not right." He tapped the instrument. "The compass isn't functioning."

"What do you mean?"

"I mean it keeps spinning. I can't get a reading. I hope it didn't get damaged when I fell."

"Maybe it's the aurora? Magnetic energy?"

"Maybe. It's weird though."

"It can join the growing list. This whole night is turning out weird. I can't—" Olivia gasped.

"Liv? What's wrong?"

"Something moved out there. Something in the trees."

"Come on, you're just imagining—" Noah gulped as a shadow flitted in the branches. "Or maybe not."

"It's probably just an owl, or an insomniac squirrel." She tried to laugh at her own joke. The weak guffaw sounded flat and hollow.

"Liv, it's moving again. It's moving fast, Liv."

She answered Noah with a scream. He shouted back as an elongated creature burst from the tree line and flew across the sky. They both ducked and tumbled into the snow, startled by the rushing thud of beating wings. Olivia glimpsed scales and feathers, and sharp claws, as it soared on barbed plumed wings. It looked like a flying snake. She sucked in air, each breath laboured as she fought against her dread and disbelief.

"What was that?"

"Just our imaginations, or a hallucination." Noah's voice trembled. "Maybe it's toxic fumes, or swamp gas." He tried to smile at her, but he only grimaced.

"Swamp gas? Noah, we're in a forest!" Panic edged into her voice. "In winter! This is bad. It could be hypothermia! Delirium or—"

Noah snorted. "Shared delirium? We both saw it, Liv. Something freaky is happening, but we aren't freezing to death. We just need to calm down, get our bearings and find our way back to camp. Simple."

"Except we're lost, and the compass isn't working, remember." She glanced upward, peering past the aurora borealis. "And do those stars look right to you? In fact, none of this," Olivia gestured, sweeping her arm across the landscape, "looks familiar. I'm scared, Noah. What's happening? Where in the world are we?"

"You aren't in your world anymore."

Noah looked at Olivia, fear consuming his eyes. "Tell me you heard that? A woman's voice?"

She nodded. They moved closer together. Olivia clutched his arm.

"I can get you home. Follow the path. Follow the light."

"What light?" Olivia snapped the question on reflex. The moment her words faded on the air a glow appeared to their right, at the edge of the trees. "Oh, that light."

She stepped over to Noah and entwined her gloved

hand in his. Her body trembled. "What's going on? What do we do?"

Noah squeezed her hand. She could hear him breathing. In and out, in and out, until he finally answered. "Maybe we listen to the spooky voice?"

"Really?" Olivia dropped his hand. His words sent a shudder of disbelief through her. "Are you crazy? We need to make a plan, assess the situation rationally, find a way back, not go off chasing voices." She took a step away from him. "I mean, it's a delusion, we're hearing things. Chasing it won't help. Chasing crazy won't help."

"I think that's exactly what will help, and I think we're past crazy, Liv. I think we've dropped into Wonderland. Right through the looking glass. Energy curtains, flying snakes, disembodied voices. It doesn't add up to normal or rational. And it isn't a delusion. We can't think our way out. We have to feel. And I feel like I can trust Miss Spooky up there. If the voice says it can get us home, I say take a chance on the voice. Besides, what are our other choices? Stay here, or wander around and hope for the best?"

"Wandering is dangerous. Staying is dangerous."

"See. Listen to the eerie woman. I say we start walking." He turned and gazed at her. His puppy dog eyes thumped against her heart. "Do you trust me?"

Olivia inhaled. "Yes."

"Then trust me. We follow the light."

With no more discussion, he strode off, heading for the woods.

"Follow him, child, before you are separated."

Realising Noah was serious—and leaving her behind—she raced after him. One way or another, they were in this madness together.

The pair slogged through the snow, a slight breeze ruffling the fur on their parkas. They reached the glow—snaking ribbons of light—and it flitted away, winding through the trees. They trailed after it.

"Good children. Follow the light. Never leave the light. It will take you home."

The shimmering streamers led down a narrow track, and they pushed through underbrush and past trees, winding further into the woods. They didn't talk, the only noise their footsteps across the snow and the occasional snap and swish of tree branches. Olivia wanted to say something, even opened her mouth to form words, but somehow she stayed silent. Inside a gnawing fear grew.

Suddenly she careened into Noah as he pulled up short.

"Why are you stopping?"

"There's a fork in the path."

"Yeah, so? Your follow-the-leader light is pointing right. We head that way."

"It's beautiful, so beautiful."

"I guess. Whatever." Olivia shuffled her feet. "Come on Noah. Move. To the right we go."

"But the aurora light is to the left."

"Huh?" As Olivia turned her head, she heard too late: *"Don't look."*

Then her mind exploded in shades of emerald and mauve, swirling colours turning on a dirge of wind-born chime. And she saw no path but the one to the left.

"Do you see it, Liv? Do you hear it? It's calling."

"Yes."

Noah took her hand and guided her towards an iridescent curtain of radiance deep in the forest.

"Oh, children. Don't go that way."

But all they heard was the wind.

⁘⸰⸰

In a strange, silent accord they trekked through the forest, unaware of anything save their destination. They ignored the branches scraping at their parkas, the feel and sound of their feet on the worn path. Primal impulses deluged their brains, steering a course to the enticement beckoning through the foliage.

"Turn back."

For a flicker, Olivia hesitated, her eyes darting to the cold, shadowy landscape behind them.

"Come on, Liv." She could hear the impatience in Noah's voice as he clasped her hand. "We have to move forward. We have to!" He tugged her arm, compelling them forward. Noah led them into the gloom, and the cover of the trees swallowed them.

The narrow, tamped-down path led a serpentine track

deeper into the forest. Trepidation irritated the edge of Olivia's mind, and part of her wanted to shout, to slow down, but neither her tongue nor her feet obeyed these nagging thoughts. Her actions seemed beyond her control. She let Noah guide their course and squeezed his hand whenever he glanced at her.

The path ended in a clearing, the snow packed by the heavy wear of feet. The aurora light surrounded it, enclosed it. To Olivia it seemed reminiscent of a nest or a cave. Near the centre she saw a large indentation in the snow and an assortment of scattered bones. Red stains littered the snow and ruptured the pale white shell of frozen ground.

Olivia released Noah's hand. Her heart pounded. A chill rose across the open space, driven from the edge of the trees. Olivia shuddered. She heard Noah whisper, "What happened?"

Wind exhaled decay across the landscape. Nausea gripped Olivia. She gagged, and beside her Noah wretched. A scritching noise drifted from the black veil of the woodland. Shuffling, advancing footsteps echoed, and the raw wind whipped the snow about in a flurry.

"Run, children, run."

"Noah?" Olivia whispered, her voice a tremble of fear.

"I don't know. I don't know. Maybe we better—"

A figure charged from the trees. Serrated teeth, sharp claws, yellow-grey skin drawn taut over four skeletal limbs barrelled at them with uncanny speed. An inhuman roar, a throaty, growling screech lobbed a bitter rage and shattered the air. It sent the pair screaming in a mad panicked dash to escape.

They veered left, headed unthinking to the closest patch of woods. Olivia pulled ahead of Noah, her mind roaring in shock and fear. She heard a soft cry and a thud, glancing back to see Noah had fallen. Olivia came to a stumbling halt and ran back to help but was too late.

The figure from the woods overtook Noah, clamping its jaws over his arm and biting down. It dragged him a few feet in the opposite direction of Olivia.

"No!"

Her shriek startled the creature and it dropped Noah. Olivia snatched up a nearby bone and swung. The makeshift club smashed against the creature's face with a satisfying crunch. It staggered but didn't fall. She swung again; this time the beast caught the end of the bone.

"Crap." Her whisper lost itself to the keening wind.

The beast wrenched Olivia sideways and jerked her off her feet. She tumbled across the snow, landing a few feet away, and cracked her head on a patch of ice. Olivia's eyelids fluttered, and her mind drifted along the edge where light and shadow melded. She teetered on the periphery of consciousness or insanity.

A voice boomed inside her head. "*Get up! Run!*"

Olivia crawled, fumbling to her feet. She heard Noah moaning, jumbling with the yowl of the wind. Through blurry vision she saw him climb to his feet, clutching his arm, and stumble toward the tree line. She choked on the smell of decay, heard the crunch of snow underfoot. A hunched figure approached; its lipless mouth salivated and dripped blood.

"*Run, you stupid girl!*"

Olivia ran.

She shoved her way through trees and brush, stumbling,

scurrying from tree to tree with one thought: escape. She pumped her legs, spraying snow in her wake until her lungs ached and her muscles throbbed in pain. Only then did her panic subside and she stopped, sucking in her breath. She looked back, scanning the woods over her shoulder, but saw nothing following her. And remembered.

"Noah!" She turned back towards the clearing but didn't see him.

"No! Don't go back! Come this way."

The disembodied voice alarmed her, and she twisted about looking for someone, anyone.

"Keep moving. Come to me. Come, I can help."

A terrified Olivia grasped at the one thread of hope in the ethereal words. "You can help me? Help me save Noah?"

"Come. I can help you. Come this way."

A dancing wisp of green light appeared in front of her nose. It darted away, towards an opening in the trees, and then hovered there. Olivia took a step and the light moved into the trees.

"Follow it."

Olivia chased the light, feeling as if she or the world had become unhinged. Stuffing away all rational thought she blundered forward until she came upon another clearing.

A bonfire blazed at the centre, a campfire where a large iron cauldron perched atop the flames. An elderly woman in a long woollen dress and gloves and wrapped in a shawl stood tending the pot. She gave whatever was inside the pot a stir and looked at Olivia.

The woman smiled. "Hello. I see you have arrived in one piece."

"Um, yeah. I guess." Olivia didn't know what else to say.

The woman hummed as she stirred her stewpot. "Would you like a taste?" The crone dipped her spoon and then held a lump of sticky grey splodge towards Olivia, who shook her head.

The woman shrugged. "No matter." She pushed the utensil back in the stew.

Olivia moved closer until she could see the wrinkles on the old woman's face. "Where am I? Are you camping here? Or do you live nearby?" The woman looked at her. The silver tinge to the crone's eyes unnerved Olivia. Then something dawned on her. "Are you the one who tried to help us?"

The old woman nodded.

"Then you know. What happened? Please, *please*. We still need help. My friend and I, we're just lost. There were lights, and a weird energy, and the compass didn't work. Then we saw *things*." A torrent of words prattled from Olivia's mouth. "But my friend's still out in the woods. And you know there's something out there with him. He needs help. We need to go find him or—or maybe call for help. Do you have a phone?" She clung to a last vestige of her reality as her pleas tumbled out, thrust by fright and distress.

"Of course not. Why would I have a phone? None of your silly technology will work here. We are beyond the realm of mortals."

"Beyond the realm?"

She's crazy. But isn't that sort of what Noah said?

"What are you babbling about? Please, we need to find my friend, Noah." Olivia glanced around, looking for a way out of the glade, but only saw a curtain of thick mist surrounding the clearing. Yellowish mist, tinged with flecks of shining emerald green and deep violet. She shuddered as her thoughts collapsed into acceptance. "Where am I?"

"Where you've always been. The forest."

Olivia shook her head. "No. This isn't the woods where we camped. This place…it's somewhere else."

"True. But it is also the same forest. You have shifted. Outside your realm and into another. In the same place but with different rules. Darker rules."

Olivia muttered under her breath. "This can't be happening, this can't be. Why do I believe this? I'll wake up, and it'll be a nightmare. Too much beer."

The old woman chuckled. "They always doubt at first. Let me introduce myself. I am Grandmother, the keeper of the forest. I am the spirit of these woods, and I can get you home."

"Home?" A tiny glint of hope kindled in Olivia's darkness. "What about Noah? I can't leave without him. Can you find him, get him home too?"

"Ah, your friend. He's a different matter. By now he belongs to the great beast of this forest. The same one you encountered."

Olivia shivered. "I didn't imagine that?" Her lower lip trembled. "It wasn't a bear or a—"

"No, my dear, it wasn't a bear."

"Then what is that thing?" Her voice was a whisper, a bare resonance gliding across the air.

"It has many names. The Mi'kmaq call it Chenu. The Iroquois named it Stonecoat, the Algonquian, Windigo."

"Wait. That last one sounds familiar."

"You may know the name better by its modern variation. Wendigo."

Olivia stared at the woman, her thoughts a dark eddy of disbelief. *That's crazy. For crap's sake a couple of my favourite shows had episodes about a Wendigo. It's fiction, a folktale, nothing more than...*

"A made-up story." Olivia tittered, an edge of her hysteria trickling out. "That's only a story."

"Yet here you are, standing next to me after an encounter with that story." The old woman threw a stick on her fire. "Stories sometimes begin with the truth. They are first told as warnings, then often end as fanciful tales.

But they still hold a truth. The Wendigo is real."

She tossed another stick on her fire and sparks snapped into the night air. "Every one of the beasts begins as a human. A person. Until the curse creeps into their heart and turns it to ice. Until they hunger, crave the taste of flesh of their own kind."

The woman sighed. "The first bite will call to them. Some do it to stave off starvation, some because they're mad, but if they continue, listen to the call, the curse will freeze their heart. Then they are lost. Then they will seek out the taste of human flesh, become a demon, a Wendigo."

"You can't be serious. You're telling me the beast eats human—Noah!" A cold, bleak pit opened in Olivia's mind. "He's still out there with that—that thing! You have to help me find Noah! I have to find him before that creature does."

"Child you don't understand. The time has passed to aid your friend. The Wendigo has him by now."

Olivia shook, her body convulsing in denial of the worst. "No, no! You're wrong! We can save him! He's still out there! I know he is! He could've made it to the woods, got away!"

The crone tilted her head and shook it slightly. "Unlikely. Even if he did, it will not matter soon. I know this beast well. No prey escapes him long, and he has chosen your friend as prey. There is much you need to see, I think, to find your answers." The old woman smiled again, a hair-raising toothy grin. "Come closer to the fire, my dear."

Despite her growing panic, Olivia felt drawn to the fire and took a few hesitant steps forward, until she could feel the searing heat on her skin. She stared at Grandmother, who began to speak.

"This Wendigo, he's an old one. Born in the winter moonlight many long years past. He was a strapping man then—young, hearty and answered to the name of François. Look upon the flames, my child, and you will know his sad tale of woe."

Olivia gazed at the roaring blaze, studying the quavering pyre as it shifted and oscillated. Her vision flickered and prickled with the orange glow, and her world shrank to the firelight. Strange images and shapes danced in that glimmer and formed a kaleidoscope-spooled narrative for Olivia to view.

A man huddled by a winter campfire, mirror to the one before her; he melted snow in a tin cup. Beside him, lying on a striped woollen blanket, rested another man. The person with the cup, the one Grandmother called François, smiled at the figure on the blanket.

"A little water will make you feel better, Jean. You'll see." He removed the cup from the flames and set it in the snow to cool a bit. Then he held the cup to his friend's lips. "Drink."

Jean lifted his head and allowed François to pour some lukewarm liquid down his throat.

"Merci. It is kind, but you and I know I am done. This fever will take me soon. And you will not be far behind, mon ami. What meagre food we had is gone, as lost as we two in these woods."

François looked away from his friend, and his features hardened, an expression of grief and resentment spilling across his face. "Yes. Losing the stores in the river was bad luck. Worse luck, this winter storm stranding us here."

"My fault, mon ami. I am sorry. I am sorry that it ends this way."

"You could not have known. You rest, Jean. Close your eyes and rest." François watched his friend fall asleep, watched his breathing even, his repose turn peaceful. Then he leaned over and picked up his hunting knife.

The flames flicked and the vision wavered, only to coalesce on another scene. It was the same man, this time cooking meat over an open fire.

Olivia frowned. The cut of meat and bone looked odd, not right somehow. She noticed scraps of plaid fabric, the same colour as Jean's shirt on the ground, and a hand poking… Olivia gagged and turned away. She fled what she saw and threw up behind a tree.

Olivia leaned against the bark for a few minutes, heaving, then rinsed her mouth with some clean snow and spit. She walked back to the fire on unsteady limbs and glowered at the old woman.

"You're telling me he ate him! This François ate his friend. That's so disgusting!" Her stomach gurgled at the thought. "But what has this got to do with anything?"

"Everything, silly girl. How do you think a Wendigo is

born?" Grandmother chuckled at Olivia's gaping expression. "Well, one of the ways. There are others."

"No, no. That's nonsense. I mean, it's icky, but the guy didn't have much choice. And there are other cases in history that it happened. You're telling me they all turned into Wendigos?"

"No, child. It is not just the eating of the forbidden flesh. He accepted the evil spirit in his heart. You saw the knife in his hand. What do you think François did with it? Do you think Jean lived the night?"

"He killed him?"

She nodded. "His action, his consumption of his friend, they called the demon Wendigo spirit and it possessed him. François brought the curse upon his own head. He is forever starving, forever looking to feed on the flesh of humans." Grandmother looked at Olivia, sorrow and sympathy etched on her face. "Do you see now? You cannot save your friend. He is but picked over bones by now."

"No! He's not! He can't be!" Olivia shouted, trying not to gag on the pictures twisting in her mind. "He could still be alive. I know him. Noah was alive when I ran. He's smart and resourceful. He would have escaped. Noah's out there injured, maybe lost in the woods, but alive. We have to find him! Save him!"

"Injured?" the crone hissed, her tongue sharpening its tone. "I did not see. How?"

"That thing bit him."

"Bitten? By the Wendigo?" The old woman clucked her tongue. "You sly beast. I did not see, I did not see. Did you hide my eyes, beast? You had other plans all along." She turned to Olivia, a cavernous sorrow in her eyes. "You must forget him, your friend. The poor, poor boy. He has been marked for a worse fate than dead and eaten."

"Worse? How is that worse than being eaten?"

"Because a Wendigo's bite retains the curse, infects the bitten. In your world, your friend might avoid succumbing to the possession, however unlikely. But here, encompassed by magic, lured by the wicked beast itself…" The old woman shook her head. "Your young friend will soon yield to its summons and succumb to the demonic spirit. I'm sorry, but he will turn. His heart will become ice, his flesh will wither and become emaciated. He will hunt these woods with the other, transformed into a wretched, ever ravenous creature stalking the forest."

Olivia balled her hands into fists and shook her head fighting back tears. "No, it's not true."

"See for yourself."

The fire blazed, and Olivia witnessed a scene emerge in the flames; the forest encampment she and Noah had stumbled upon earlier. A gaunt fair-haired figure crouched in the snow next to a blue parka and dressed in a flannel shirt. A shirt Olivia recognised. His fingers grasped the end of a meaty bone, his teeth gnawing at the flesh. The vision wavered as the flames flickered, then his head turned and Olivia saw his face.

"Noah!"

The images faded with her gasp.

"You can see, he has already turned, your friend. He already feasts on the tainted meat of a human being, food from the Wendigo's cache. He is beyond saving."

"No. There must be something I can do! This isn't happening!"

"It is, and you must accept his fate. Forget him and worry about yourself."

The woman pressed a spherical object in her hand. Olivia glanced down. She held a mottled grey stone egg. The object felt lighter than it should, as if it was hollow.

"You must leave this place before you join your friend, either as one of them or as their dinner. Follow the path to the stone pillar and then smash the egg I've given you against its rock. That will open the doorway. The rest is up to you."

"Path? What path? What are you—" Olivia stopped speaking, her mouth agape as the crone, the fire, her whole surroundings vanished. She looked down at her feet and saw a dirt path leading north through the woods. A glance over her shoulder showed her the coal-black darkness of the forest. When she tried to turn, step away from the path, she couldn't move. She wiggled her foot, and moved it forward with no restriction. The sound of rustling leaves caught her attention, and she looked towards the forest. For a moment she bloomed with hope.

Noah! He escaped. The vision wasn't true.

But nothing save a swirling breeze left the dark forest. The wind gusted, churned around Olivia, tousling the fur on the hood of her parka, murmuring in her ear with the voice of the crone.

"Go you foolish girl, go. Go and live. Stay and die."

She sighed and bowed her head. Her heart bleeding regret and guilt, Olivia followed the path onward.

·:·

Olivia tried to keep track of how long she walked, but it became too difficult; time seemed to blend into itself. She put one aching foot in front of the other, trudging past tree after tree, feeling the crunch of snow and ice underfoot until she wanted to scream. Or cry. She kept telling herself it was a nightmare and she would wake up in the tent.

When the tree cover broke, she found herself in a small dell. She half scrambled, half slid down the side of a slight, icy hillock to the bottom of the vale. In its centre stood a pillar made of intricately stacked stones, each rock inscribed with petroglyphs and symbols. She stepped closer and ran her hand along the stone. The surface tingled under her fingertips.

As she moved her hand away, a light dusting of snow floated from the sky, the flakes drifting in the wind. A breeze that also carried the smell of decay. Olivia spun around. From the forest shadows and the snowfall he appeared, silhouetted on the edge of the small hill.

Noah.

Or at least his revenant.

Olivia gasped. Only tufts of his curly blond hair remained on his head, his skin pulled against his bones, its colour altered to a sickly looking ashen. He wore no jacket or boots, no clothing save a few tatters of a shirt on his back, and shreds of denim covering his pelvic area. He grinned at her, a queasy parody of his smile crafted from decaying and bloody lips stretched across jagged teeth.

"Leaving without me?" His formerly sweet, laughing voice came out a rasp, a harsh croak.

"Oh, Noah!" Olivia reached out to him in one last desperate effort to do something. "I'm so sorry. So sorry for what's happened." She choked back tears. "I don't know how to fix it. I don't think I can fix it."

For a flicker, his face changed, and Olivia saw the Noah she knew. For a stranded thread of time, his pleading eyes brimmed in unshed tears. "It's too late for me, Liv. Go. Before it's too late for you. He's coming."

Olivia jumped back as Noah lifted his head and howled, a raw agonized sound. Then he grasped his stomach and doubled over in pain. Noah moaned, his body shaking. He hissed through his teeth. "Run."

She took a step towards the pillar but hesitated, her eyes still staring at Noah. A moment later he raised his head and returned her gaze.

His tongue flicked across his lips. "I'm so hungry. So hungry."

His eyes shone with a scarlet light and a stare that terrified her. Behind Noah, the air shivered, and a dark humanoid shape moved forward out of the forest mist.

"Join us, Olivia."

All hesitation dissolved from Olivia in that instant.

She dashed forward and smashed the egg against the stone pillar, hard enough to jar her arm. The egg fractured into a dozen pieces, ejecting a glorious radiance to illuminate the surrounding forest. She heard a scream, an inhuman roar of hatred and fury, and the frozen ground beneath her feet cracked and convulsed. Emerald and violet light danced, streaming away from her, blazing a trail forward. More light appeared in the distance, revealing an opening. She scuttled up an embankment and ran.

Her feet sprayed snow, her speed spurred by the grunts and scrabbling noises behind her, keeping time with her pounding heartbeat. Olivia could see it now, a shimmering portal sheathed by a mini aurora borealis—her world waiting on the other side. She leapt the last small distance, flinging herself through the radiant doorway, tumbling into safety.

She looked back; her last sight before the portal closed were the gnashing crimson fangs of the Wendigo. She shivered, part from fright, part from the cold. She stared at the sunlight as it glistened off the ice-covered trees and realised with shock it was no longer night.

How long was I gone?

She found herself sprawled in front of her tent, back at her camp, so she scrambled inside. Olivia grabbed her phone, checked the date and gasped.

Three days. I was there for three days.

Her mind jumbled, she automatically checked for service, meaning to call for help, and then faltered. She wandered back outside, staring at the horizon.

How do I explain why Noah's not…

A lump formed in her throat.

He's gone. My friend, at least the man I knew, is gone. What do I say? How do I explain what happened?

She stared at the phone. Through the trees, the wind gusted, whispering to her.

"People disappear in this forest all the time. Especially in winter. Tell them he's lost."

Lost. The word tumbled around in her head. *Lost to a curse. Lost to this world, he's lost everything he knew, everything he wanted. Noah's lost…*

Reality smashed down on her like a cartoon anvil. Olivia

gagged, fell to her knees and spewed. Her insides heaved air and bile, staining the snow bilious hues of pea green and ochre. Her body shuddered, and collapsed, her muscles and bones curling into a fetal position.

She cried. For Noah, for herself, for all the lost that came before, and all that would come after. The wailing wind echoed her despondent sobs, and somewhere, beyond the ken of this world, a newborn Wendigo howled.

Courser

Aeryi huddled against the brick wall, pressed into a dim and dingy corner of a backstreet alley. Danger stalked the hours after the twelfth bell chimed. Creatures—beasts both otherworldly *and* mortal—emerged from shadowed streets to hunt. She shivered, the echo of her dead father's voice ringing in her head.

"Never be a victim, child. Never."

Footsteps echoed from the front of the alley where it met the street. A husky voice sang a shanty song off-key, and a burly drunken sailor stumbled down towards Aeryi. From her hiding place, she smelled his sweat and the stink of fish mixed with cheap liquor.

"Hey. Is someone back there?" The man stopped, swaying on his feet, and peered into the shadows.

Damn, he's spotted me. Not the best timing, but it will have to do.

Aeryi smiled, a cold, lifeless salute, and leapt from her hiding place in a diving roll. She slashed her knife with practised ease. Her prey, the poor drunkard, screamed and fell on the cobblestones, his calf half-severed and bleeding. In one swift motion she sprang to her feet, staring down at the injured man. His blood dripped from her knife onto the stony ground.

"Come and feed," she whispered, and the alley swirled with black pulsing mist.

She watched the air solidify as pale hunched-over creatures cloaked in ebon smoke and incorporeal substance shuffled from the dark night. She watched as the unnatural things gravitated to the groaning man, who wriggled on the stones, still unaware of his fate. Her father's voice again whispered in her ear.

"Sometimes a devil's bargain is all you have."

Some part of her wanted to look away, but she kept her gaze straight ahead on the unfolding scene. The beings swarmed the poor unfortunate soul with gnashing teeth and slicing claws.

"What are you? Get away! Stay away! No, no, please, no!"

The drunk's shrieks filled the alley as his death surrounded him. They paid no heed to his screams and pleas for mercy; they thought only of their meal. In sloppy gulps and licking tongues their razor teeth devoured flesh and bone, drank of bile and blood, until not a scrap of body remained.

One turned to Aeryi then, a ragged-toothed smile peeking from an eternal black emptiness with red eyes that swirled in unknown emotion. "Good hound." A raspy semblance of a voice addressed her. "Find good meat." It raised its facsimile of a limb and patted her head with blood-stained claws. Only experience and practice prevented Aeryi from shuddering. "Now find more. Still hungry."

"Yes, master. As you command." She gave a slight bow. "Another kill tonight. I'll find you someone."

Another smile and the thing and its fellows melted

back into the shadows. Aeryi headed into the street to find another victim for the beasts that controlled her. The echo of her father's voice followed her as she stalked the town, her mind full of the words he spoke the day he bound her body and soul to the creatures.

"One day you'll understand. One day you'll thank me. This way you'll be safe. This way you'll be strong. Better to be predator than prey."

Whispers caught her attention. A man and a woman under a shaded awning beside an alley. She smiled.

Fresh meat.

She slithered forward to find a concealed vantage point, hiding in the night's embrace, waiting, watching. Her gaze followed the man's hands as they moved over the woman's body, studied their lips as they pressed together in a kiss. Memories stirred of the first boy she kissed. She had enjoyed the moment, but not what came after. No, she did not enjoy seeing her father's knife cut the boy's throat. She remembered screaming, being held by her father, made to watch her friend bleed out and die.

Most of all she remembered the whispers in her ear. "Emotion will kill you. Love will weaken you. It will make you vulnerable."

Is that how you felt about Mother?

The almost forgotten memory of a face surfaced—a warm smile and kind eyes. Aeryi remembered being happy then. Her father laughed when her mother lived with them.

Did he love her then? Did she love him? It couldn't have lasted. Not at the end.

Aeryi watched the lovers on the street, playing the questions over in her head along with the images of her mother's last days. The look of betrayal, her screams as men dragged her from the house. She never saw her again.

Traded to pay Father's gambling debts. Sold off without a second thought. That was the day he changed. The day the obsession started.

The couple's laughter brought her back to the now. They moved deeper into the alley, out of her line of sight. She uncoiled from her crouching position and went on the move, silently crossing the street to skulk behind a wooden barrel and view her targets. She paused, senses alert, but the couple were too busy with each other to notice anything else.

She settled in, enjoying her voyeuristic view of the couple's amorous pursuits, the flash of skin, their moans and cries of pleasure. She could have moved in and taken them down, but it didn't seem right to end their lives before they were through with each other.

Let them have one last moment of happiness before the end.

Inwardly she sighed, her gut twisting in regret and sorrow.

I could walk away. Find someone else.

Her father's disapproving face flickered in her mind and she heard his words, one of the many lessons he drilled into her head: "*Never let sentiment stop you. To survive, you must be stronger than the rest of the world. You must be ruthless. The weak succumb to temptation. The weak betray. The weak die. Never be weak.*"

I'm not. I'll never be weak. Not like he was. He wasn't even strong enough to bind himself to my masters. He thought using me instead would protect him. That I would be his shield, keep him safe.

Aeryi clenched her jaw and readied her knife. There would be no reprieve for the pair in the alley. She waited until they finished, until they were fixing their clothing, before she darted forward along the shadows, knife ready to strike.

They never saw her coming.

Two slashes with the blade and it was over. The woman shrieked, her abdomen sliced open, blood gushing over skirts. She slid along the wall and collapsed. Aeryi cut deeper with the man, twisting the blade as she pulled it along his flesh. He fell to his knees trying to hold his guts inside his body.

She shouted, "Come and feed."

Aeryi stood there, waiting for the shadows to swirl, her thoughts again dwelling on her father, about his words. About the one thing he made her learn.

Always better to be predator than prey.

He was right about that one thing. He made her the perfect predator. Aeryi stepped back as she watched her masters descend on the couple, the pair nothing more than prey.

That is what it comes down to, doesn't it, Father?

Survival. What you taught me. Whatever it takes. Betray anyone to survive.

Her memories flickered, and thoughts of her father's last moments surfaced. She savoured the memory of cutting him, of calling her masters to feed on him.

Her father's dying screams were his best lesson.

The Price of Wishes

I felt her stumbling through the woods, sensed her thoughts, and she caught my attention immediately; she was looking for my well, for me. A shiver ran through me. A human seeking me out to improve her life. That hadn't happened in years.

The day might prove amusing after all.

Curious and wanting to be prepared, I probed deeper into her mind. It wouldn't hurt to take a peek. I found much of what I expected: dissatisfaction, resentment, but also sorrow and a longing to be loved. Pity surfaced, and I felt a sudden affinity for her. I too knew the pangs of loneliness. The world could be cruel to females, even such as me.

I shifted through more of her thoughts and found her name, Marion, as well as her family history. A family I knew well. I smiled.

So I showed her the right path, the hidden trail winding deeper into the forest. If she took it, she would find my well and we would see. The silly girl hesitated but followed the route I revealed, coming at last to my glade.

She spun around and clapped her hands, in some foolish dance, all human emotions. A giddy one, this Marion. I watched her run forward, skirts gathered and dark hair flying, to lean against the edge of the stone and gaze down into my water. I rippled the black murkiness and reflected her face back at her.

"Now what? Do I just make a wish or drop a coin?"

I wanted to answer her, but from that I was forbidden. The humans had to find the way on their own.

I saw her take a breath, close her eyes, and make her wish.

"I want to be noticed like my sister."

That surprised me. I expected some love request or a wish to be beautiful. Not that she wasn't already, but these human women… Yet she only wanted to be noticed. Her wish might have broken my heart if I still had one.

I delayed a few beats and she opened her eyes. I saw the look of disappointment and smiled. Always make them wait for the drama. I then swirled the wind around the well and sprayed a splash of water up from the depths. I lowered my voice and echoed it across the glade.

"So be it."

I watched the woman screech and jump back, afraid. I suppressed a laugh. She glanced around, jerking her head, trying to see who spoke, acting skittish. She backed away before turning and running down the path as if a monster chased her. I followed her, still invisible, and she sprinted back to the main trail. She stopped, panting for breath. With a bit of mischief in my soul, I made the path to my well vanish. With another screech she bolted, I presumed back to her village. This time I chuckled.

And then I was alone again.

I sighed and returned to my well. As annoying as it was to grant the humans these mundane wishes, they were the only contact I had with other living beings. No animals ventured into the glade; the magic tied to this place scared them. Even birds avoided flying overhead. This Marion had been the first creature I'd seen in decades. Her wish had been interesting at least. I hoped she'd enjoy it. I hoped even more she'd return.

After three days of staring at the same sky, wandering the same circle of trees, I saw Marion return to the woods. I revealed the hidden trail once more, eager to see want she wanted now. I could sense greed in her thoughts and I liked that. I could work with that. And at least she would be a diversion from the boredom.

Soon she stood at the edge of the well once more, looking down into the dark waters. Her hands gripped the edge of the stone as she rambled words. "I don't know how, but whatever magic you did worked. People are being kind and sweet to me, and my family pays attention to me instead of being dismissive. It's… I want more. I want another wish." She licked her lips and said, "I want to have money. Enough for fine dresses and fancy jewellery."

A step up for this one, is it? And a more challenging wish that would need a bit of finesse. I reached out into the world, searching for the right threads to pull. Ah, there. A rich aunt. Just a change here, and here, and an unfortunate death to make it happen. I tweaked reality with my magic and set the consequences to play out.

Then, with a touch of drama again, I answered in a breath of wind and a swirl of water, "So be it."

I smiled as Marion skipped away. I wondered how she would react to what I had done. Would she be appalled or return for more wishes? I secretly hoped she would come back. She could be so useful.

⁘

I didn't see Marion for several more months, but when she returned, she had a look of desperation in her eyes. She had embraced her last wish to be certain, as her clothes were much finer quality than before. What did she desire now?

She leaned on the well, leather gloves pressing against the stone. "I don't know what you are, but can you help me? I have everything I asked for, but I'm still not happy. Why isn't my life complete? I'm rich, I'm well-respected, yet... What else do I need to wish for?"

Interesting. No wish, but a plea for help. This Marion was a fascinating human and a desirous one. Time to test her resolve with my own little twist. "I can grant you the happiness you seek. In exchange for a favour." I held my breath. Would this work?

Marion shivered. "A favour? Why?"

Not an outright refusal. Good. "Is it so much to ask a wish of my own? I serve those in need, grant them their wishes. I have given you all you have asked."

"True, but I am still unhappy." Marion stared into the water. "You don't seem very good at it."

I bristled. Hardly my fault humans aren't easily satisfied. I tempered my anger, replying, "I am bound by what you asked of me."

"I suppose." Marion sighed. "So how do I know what to ask this time?"

A flash of annoyance shot through me. Silly girl with her indecision. Must I walk her to the answer? "Don't you know the source of your unhappiness?"

She sighed again. "I'm all alone. All my friends have husbands or beaus. My sister is about to wed, but I have no one. I have money and I'm pretty enough. Why won't a man look at me the way that stupid blacksmith's apprentice looks at my sister, Edith?"

Finally. "I can make that happen."

"How? I thought magic couldn't force love?"

Who has this human been talking to? "Untrue. I can bring you the man of your dreams. You can have the happiness you seek. I can give you everything." I hesitated a heartbeat and added, "I only require a small favour and you will have your heart's desire."

"You can truly do that? Give me love?"

Yes, she took the bait. "I can. Just grant me the favour."

I watched the woman frown. *Oh dear. Have I lost her?*

"That sounds…tempting, but it's just… I know nothing of who you are, what you are. Doing you a favour without knowing… What if you're trying to trick me? I'll only consider it if you tell me what kind of creature you are."

Now she gets squeamish about dealing with magical beings? And of course I'm trying to trick you, you foolish thing. Time to lie, I suppose, and add a few theatrics.

"I am fae, a water sprite." I swirled the well water upward into a funnel, moulding it into the shape of a buxom female water nymph. Hopefully it would fool her long enough.

Marion gasped and jerked herself backwards. "Oh my. A nymph? You're good creatures, I guess. My granny never spoke badly of you, anyway."

Inwardly I sneered. I knew her granny. The woman had been a hateful bitch with no qualms about using me for her wishes, even after… Best not to dwell on that but instead focus on Marion.

I took a breath and said, "So you'll help me?" I made my water nymph speak my words, even put a bit of sad pleading in her eyes.

Marion inhaled and exhaled a slow breath. "What do you need?"

Yes! I had her. *Careful now, don't spook her.*

"Do you know the Ruin of Nerael?"

Marion nodded and replied, "That broken stone building in the hills above the village?"

"Yes, that's the one." *Careful, not too eager.* "Fetch me a piece of embedded quartz from the stone, bring it here and drop it in the water."

"Is that all?" She seemed surprised. "I expected something more difficult or horrible. Why would you need a piece of old rock?"

I fell silent. Marion was proving difficult. Perhaps I needed a bit of truth mixed with another lie. "I want to be free. I am chained to this well by an evil curse. If you bring me the quartz, I can break the curse."

Marion furrowed her brow. "How is a piece of stone going to do that?"

Really? This human was exasperating.

"Do you care?" I snapped the words without thinking.

But Marion furrowed her brow and surprised me. "You're right, I don't. If you want to be free, then I suppose it doesn't matter how. I'll get you the silly rock, but I want what you promised in return."

I wanted to laugh out loud but said, "A deal, then. One that needs to be sealed. A drop of your blood in the well, if you please. There's a sharp stone inside the well, just below the edge."

"Eww." Marion wrinkled her nose but peered into the well and located the stone. She pricked her finger and a drop of her blood fell in the water. The ground quivered and I smiled.

"It is done. Bring me what I ask and you will have the love you seek."

Marion left and my heart sang with joy.

After a few anxious days she returned to me. I felt the power of the quartz she carried the moment she entered the woods, and all my worry disappeared. Marion kept her word. I watched her enter the glade, anticipation tingling through every ounce of my essence.

She strode to the well and shouted, "I'm here! I have the silly rock."

I blew a gentle wind around the well. "Drop the quartz in the water, please."

Marion dug the stone out of a pocket, held it over the water and released it. The piece of crystal fell with a satisfying plop, descending deep into the well. I felt its magic meld with the curse the moment it touched the surface, and within seconds the spell binding me to this place snapped.

As I surged from my prison, coming back into the mortal world on a voluminous plume of smoke, memories flooded back. Of being betrayed by the human wizard I loved, of the years I searched for him and his spell crystal. Memories of the grief and anger I had felt when I found the villagers had killed him and embedded his broken crystal in the walls of Nerael. I vented all my pain and triumph in a tree-rattling shriek and rode the sooty haze back into the mortal realm.

As the smoke coalesced and my shout subsided, I materialized beside the well in my true form: a creature of flames, vaguely human-looking, with dark-blue skin and piercing emerald eyes.

"I am free! At long last, unchained from that accursed well!" I bowed to Marion. "I thank you."

She stared, aghast, and stammered, "You—you're not Fae, you're a—a—"

"Djinn. Yes, I know, I lied. But I'll still keep my word and give you what you want."

"You tricked me, you lying little—wait. You'll still help me?"

"A bargain is a bargain, Marion. You granted me a favour and I'll grant you happiness." I closed my eyes and reached out. *Ah, there he is, the perfect man.* The air crackled with my full power as I fulfilled her last wish.

I grinned. "Go home, my dear. Love will come knocking at your door within three days."

"It better." Marion stalked off, leaving me dancing for joy in the clearing.

I was free and my exuberance knew no bounds. I revelled in my emancipation but knew there were still things to do. My gaze fell for a moment on Marion's retreating figure, and I felt a twinge of regret. She wouldn't like what came next, even if she got her wish. Perhaps I would leave her a few weeks of happiness before I finished what I had planned. A small gift before I bestowed a lifetime of consequence.

Then again, Marion didn't seem one to dwell in guilt. Still, a small delay in my revenge wouldn't cause any harm.

⁙

I attended Marion's wedding, albeit as an invisible spirit. It was a lovely affair and she seemed happy. Her husband owned a lovely manor house nestled in the hills above her village, and they moved in there after they married.

She'd have a bird's-eye view of what I planned.

I could not exact revenge against my false love, the lying wizard who imprisoned me, but I could wreak destruction on the descendants of those vile humans who hired him. The village where Marion grew up. They were the ones who wanted a pet Djinn, the ones who used me for centuries to grant their wishes and then abandoned me. They left me to rot, imprisoned in a well, with no thought to my suffering. I would not be quite that cruel. They would suffer, but it would be brief.

I landed in the village square in a whirlwind of fire and unleashed my power. Rivers of flames lashed outward, igniting the entire village: houses and people. Smoke, screams and a firestorm raged to the sky with me at its centre. As the conflagration burned, I turned my senses to the manor house on the hill, saw Marion at the window, a look of horror etched on her face. I smiled, my last twist of vengeance ready to be enacted.

Her family had been the worst offenders over the years. They treated me as their own personal wish granter until her sanctimonious grandfather decided I was evil and forbade the villagers from visiting the well.

I closed my eyes, sending a whisper across the distance into her ear. "Do you like my handiwork?"

She answered, her voice quavering. "What have you done? Why? All those innocent people. My family."

Perhaps she had a conscience after all. Good. "What *we've* done, my dear. You set me free after all. In exchange for your last wish. And the price of wishes is always high."

I smiled as she collapsed against the window, shrieking.

Thank you for reading this book and I hope you enjoyed it. Also, please consider taking the time to leave an honest review. Authors appreciate reader feedback. If you'd like to know more about me or my books, please drop me a line at my website, Welcome to Avalon.

You can also sign up for my newsletter for regular updates on my books.

More Books by A. F. Stewart

Poetry:

Horror Haiku and Other Poems

Horror Haiku Pas de Deux

Places of Poetry

Colours of Poetry

Reflections of Poetry

Shadows of Poetry

Tears of Poetry

Multi-Author Anthologies:

Hell's Empire: Tales of the Incursion

Abandon: 13 Tales of Impulse, Betrayal, Surrender, and Withdrawal

A Twist of Fate: A Collection of 11 Twisted Fairy Tales

Beyond the Wail

Legends and Lore

Mechanized Masterpieces

Christmas Lites Series (Books III–IX)

Coffin Hop: Death by Drive-In

Fiction:

Ghosts of the Sea Moon (Saga of the Outer Islands Book I)

Souls of the Dark Sea (Saga of the Outer Islands Book II)

Renegades of the Lost Sea (Saga of the Outer Islands Book III)

Chronicles of the Undead

Killers and Demons

Killers and Demons II: They Return

Fairy Tale Fusion

Gothic Cavalcade

Ruined City

About the Author

A steadfast and proud sci-fi and fantasy geek, A. F. Stewart was born and raised in Nova Scotia, Canada and still calls it home. The youngest in a family of seven children, she always had an overly creative mind and an active imagination. She favours the dark and deadly when writing—her genres of choice being dark fantasy and horror—but she has been known to venture into the light on occasion. As an indie author she's published novels, novellas and story collections, with a few side trips into poetry.